WHEN I LOOK AT THE SKY, ALL I SEE ARE STARS

STEVE STRED

BLACK VOID PUBLISHING

Ebook and Paperback cover art by Greg Chapman

Hardcover cover art by Kristina at Truborn

Edited by David Sodergren

Ebook ISBN: 9781990260377

Paperback ISBN: 9781990260384

Hardcover ISBN: 9781990260391

ADVANCE PRAISE

'FROM PHILOSOPHY TO SPIRITUALITY and all the complicated weigh-stations in-between, Steve Stred's *'When I Look At the Sky, All I See Are Stars,'* is a gore-soaked psychosexual possession story sure to leave you breathless, both from the full-on assault of the author's gift for splatter and suspense, but also in anticipation of whatever he does next.'

— Kealan Patrick Burke, Bram Stoker Award-winning author of *Kin* and *Sour Candy*.

*

'Steve Stred unleashes a full throttle terror that will delight readers of both possession and cosmic horror. This one torched my eyeballs!'

— Tim McGregor, author of *Eynhallow*, *Wasps in the Ice Cream* and *Lure*

*

'Stred's best work yet! A psychosexual nightmare that only gets darker as the mystery unfolds.'

— Duncan Ralston, author of *Woom* and *Ghostland*

*

'A deeply unsettling read. 'When I Look At the Sky, All I See Are Stars' is a fever dream of madness, violence, possession, death, and what comes afterwards. Steve Stred approaches each act of horror with near sadistic glee, dragging us from one nightmarish set piece to the next, racing towards a pitch-black finale.'

- C.M. Forest, author of *Infested*

*

'A deliciously malevolent slice of cosmic horror. Sinister and unrelenting, it breathlessly propels you into the unknown.'

- Evan Dickson, screenwriter, *V/H/S/85* and *Totem*

READER WARNING

The following story is based on real events, or, more accurately, a real interaction.
Readers please be advised.
From the Fall of 2018 until the Spring of 2021, I joined a cult on the dark web to
research the three novellas that comprised my Father of Lies Trilogy.
My time spent within that 'community' was a fascinating look into the search for
belonging and the lengths some people will go in hopes of discovering a higher
power and a different place beyond the life we know.
I have been forever changed, re-shaped by this experience, and have had to deal
with how the time spent within that headspace has affected my real, day-to-day
life.
It is not something I suggest you attempt.

For those of blackness and covered in ash.
Thank you for letting me spend time with you.
I hope, wherever you are, you've found,
What it is you were looking for.

The Book of Lies
Book One: Birth
1:3 for the blackness would swirl and the stars would anguish
*

'But we made a pact based on darkness.
And when I look at the sky, all I see are stars.'
@beggingfortheash, Dark Web Cult Member
November 2018

Part One
Beginning

1.

THE FIRST LETTER I ever read from him.

This is it.

It's strange.

Hard to read, hard to process, tough to digest when I know who he was and what he was capable of.

Did you want to read it?

No?

Why not?

Please, I insist. It'll help you understand him and me. Or is it I whom you need to understand?

Where did I find this? I found it in an old box, stuffed away in a strange little chest. I didn't know this was where all her stuff was.

It was addressed to *David*...

I hate that name. It doesn't mean anything to me anymore. Just a label. A way for you to catalog me in here and out there.

Oh, sorry, spaced out a bit there, didn't I?

Anyways, so it was in this old box, stuffed behind a trunk of faded jeans that stunk of old cigarettes.

I sat cross-legged. Pulled it out. Wondered what it was.

Faded yellow. I remember that most of all. As though they'd been hidden for centuries, not years. Delicate, that was for sure. The first envelope I pulled from the stack was clumped together with the others by an old, cracked rubber band that quickly broke.

Was it addressed to anyone?

Yeah. Me. Just my name. Horrible handwriting. Worse than my own. But that's the curse of the computer age people, isn't it? No one's able to use a pen or pencil. Cursive has become extinct.

What did I do?

I stared at it for a minute. I knew I was crying; I could feel the tears on my face, which was odd. I'm usually emotionless. I had to wipe them away. I was scared a tear would fall and ruin this artifact I held in my hands.

Ten minutes, I'd say. About that. Before I was able to get my finger under the tiny sliver of tape that'd been used to seal it. A single sheet of faded lined paper fluttered out.

Oh, you want me to read it to you now?

What's changed?

That's fair. Progress is always good.

This is what it said.

2.

DR. RACHEL HOGGENDORF STOOD on the other side of the one-way mirror that adorned the wall of the intake interview room, and watched with fascination.

Her newest patient, David Stewart, sat alone in the room, but since he'd been escorted in and had his handcuffs affixed to the table, he hadn't shut up.

She'd dealt with a number of patients suffering from multiple-personality disorder, but never once had any of them acted the way David was acting.

Rachel was considered a rising star in the world of Psychology. Only thirty-seven, she was single with no children, and spent anywhere from sixteen to twenty hours a day at the institute. She had a driving focus – being the best in her field and making the most significant difference in her patients' lives that she could – and because of that focus, she didn't spend much time outside of work cultivating friendships. She didn't care about that. What she cared about, and what motivated her, were the people in here, one of whom was currently speaking as though they were being interviewed by someone elsewhere.

"Any trouble getting him in the room?"

Rachel looked over at the bulky older man who had entered.

Harvey Wilson was the Chief of Staff at the institute. At sixty-three, he'd worked at the institution over half his life. While he was clean-shaven, he was almost completely bald, with only a small scruff of grey hair lightly growing around the sides of his head. Why he kept it, no one knew, but Rachel always assumed it was a matter of personal pride. Since his wife had died unexpectedly almost three years ago, Harvey had put on close to seventy-five pounds, all of it carried in his stomach.

"Hey, Harv. No, not that I was told."

"I always marvel at the multi-personality folks. You think the one sitting there knows they killed someone?"

"What makes you so sure he has multiple?" Rachel asked, watching as David grew animated, despite being unable to stand due to the cuffs.

"Just going by what his chart says. Why's he look so familiar?"

"He looks like that actor from Beverly Hills 90210. I keep messing up his name, thinking it's David Silver, not David Stewart," Rachel said, smiling.

"Never watched it. But you're right, he does look like that actor. Just shorter. Bit more unhinged," he said with a chuckle.

Rachel wasn't one to comment on her patients, and she wasn't about to start now. She knew that was how Harvey liked to operate, keeping things light-hearted and full of 'positive energy' as he called it. Still, she wanted to focus on what David was saying. These moments, the unguarded moments, were the times they often spoke without a filter, and she wanted to observe as much of it as she could.

She watched as he began to speak again.

*

'I never thought I'd be what I am. Guess I'm writing this 'cuz I don't trust people and I ain't gonna share what's going on up here with them out there. Listen, maybe one day you'll read this. And if you do, I want you to know a few things. I'll try my best. I really will. I'm a hard worker. Strong hands. Muscles built on hard labor over the years. Tough. I know these aren't the greatest traits to share with your unborn, but you need to know that no matter what life throws my way, our way, it can't keep me down. When you're old enough, you'll learn what I mean and why it's important. Your, Dad.'

*

How did reading that make me feel?

Like I said, I'm emotionless usually, but seeing how it was signed...

Yeah, that got me.

There were more.

How many?

Maybe fifty or so.

Did I read 'em all?

Yeah. Some were nonsense. Some were ramblings. A few were along the lines of that first one.

Which were my favorites?

The ones where he described things we did together.

I don't remember a lot when it comes to things we did together.

I wish I did.

Do you remember things you did with your parents?

No, no... I understand, this isn't about you. Just making small talk. It's tough when you don't have friends to make small talk with.

Is it raining out? Sunny?

I get it, you won't answer me. I'll answer for myself.

Probably sunny. Slight breeze. People walking around, enjoying their lives, knowing they're free and that under their feet is solid ground and above their heads is the bluest sky.

You want me to share a few of the letters that describe things we did together?

Oh yes, oh absolutely.

No, you don't need to send someone to get the box. I can remember every single word.

I like this one quite a bit, but it's not my favorite.

I can share that one after, if you'd like.

*

'Well, today was a journey. Some might've considered it a confluence of things going wrong. But not me. It's always a joy to just be out among the people, and to see what the different walks of life are up to. I'm not rich, but I've found it's easy enough to pretend to be someone who has money in the bank. Just go walk through the lobbies of fancy hotels. Mingle where the rich folk park their cars on the street. Find a free outdoor festival and participate as able.

Today, we went to the outdoor concert series in the park. I was able to get us close enough that we could see the band on the stage, but we didn't have to pay for seating in the grass. I loved it. I'd never heard the band before, but they had people up and moving. I love to watch people dance. To see them swaying and joining in together with a shared rhythm. A few of the people beside us wanted to get us dancing too. I did, but I'm not so good with being that close to people, especially when the women don't have much clothing on.

After the band was done, some horrible group came on, preaching and telling people to bow their heads to say some words together to the Lord above. I would've spit on the singer if we were closer.

Instead, we walked around the tents that were set up, selling different food and crafts. A few places had free samples, so we didn't even need to pay to have a few snacks. Not that I'd brought any money. I went back to a couple; they didn't recognize us the second time around. I knew they wouldn't, but some people have a keen eye. Can see beyond what's offered.

On the walk home, we sat on a bench as the night sky opened and we just stared in silence for a while. There's so much up there, out there, when you stop and allow it to come into you. Not many people know how though.

Not many will allow it.'

*

No, I'm not crying. It's just such a beautiful thing to remember.

And it's true, you know?

Not many people know how to allow the power of the cosmos to enter and flow through their bodies. We learned at a young age. My dad was taught by a fella down the road.

They played music together and drank moonshine and smoked until the sun came up.

Those were good times. It was sad when he died. He'd found the path in his life that made him happy and when he strayed, he didn't last long.

That's the key, isn't it? To a healthy life. Find your path.

Have I found mine?

I believe so. Some may say it's not the path I should be on, or the path they'd choose, but that's on them.

Each person should be happy.

They should be free to love who they love.

Oh, yeah? I agree. Life's so fleeting. We should just be happy, right?

True.

Some do choose chaos, and that's a horrible way to go about your day.

Anarchy and anti-establishment and harassment.

Am I being sarcastic?

No. Maybe? Yes? But no.

I'm hard to follow? You don't need to be rude. I'm not being rude. I'm not talking down to you or treating you like any less of an individual. No, no. I'm simply here, answering your questions.

You've not asked a question?

Hmmm.

*

Sure, crowds can be overwhelming, but they have their benefits, especially if you're looking to do something and remain unobserved.

I, for one, also do enjoy a simple one-on-one interaction. You can really get to know a person through that sort of contact. See in their eyes. Know what's going on behind them.

I met a man today down near the old burned-out house that the Christiansons used to live in. I often wander near there, exploring, enjoying the solitude and silence it offers. He was older than me, and I could tell he was wise just by the glint in his eyes and the creases that adorned his face.

He told me his name, one I've forgotten many times over, and we talked.

I asked him where he was going. He said from over there, through here, and that way. You see, a man who knows his path. His direction. He asked the same of me and I found my answer to not be so simple. He replied that he understood and that because some of us are put here, in this place, for a specific reason, it was only natural that my path ventured in an un-straight line.

After a while, we both marveled at the complexity of us and of them and how when the two combine, the circle becomes complete.'

*

No, I don't speak in riddles.

Nor does he. Nor they. Nor them.

We all speak as we see fit, as befits us.

As a scholar to a student.

As a student to a peer.

As a peer to a rat.

It's a delicate balance and we're here to not upset that balance.

3.

"THINK I'LL LEAVE YOU to keep tabs on him," Harvey said. He walked to the doorway and stopped. "When are you going to go in? Introduce yourself."

"I think I'll watch until he peters out. He's been going at such a frantic pace, there's gotta be a lag coming soon."

"Sounds good, Rachel. Holler if you need anything." He tucked his hands into his pockets and left her. She found it comforting that he'd not only checked in on her, but that he'd left the door open. The common sounds of the people out in the hallway and at the nursing station seeped in, letting her know she wasn't completely alone.

Looking back, she shuddered, seeing David's eyes focused directly on her, even though she knew he wasn't able to see her.

*

Was this morning rough?

Maybe.

More accurate would be calling it difficult.

Do I get along with others?

Yes. No. Maybe?

Depends.

That reminds me of an old joke my Father used to tell me. Would you like to hear it?

No?

How come?

Or does this fall into the 'no small talk' rule you arbitrarily implemented?

How about a story? You know what? Even if you don't want to hear it, I'm going to share it. This is a story he passed on. My Father would never hear it, never let me speak of it to him, but he found it of great importance, and even noted it in a letter he left behind.

*

'*Many know of the famous stories where Good overcame Evil. What if I told you there was an incident where a mighty battle took place and only one person survived? Would you still believe the story happened, if only a singular voice could profess the truth?*'

*

That's how he opened his letter to me, before retelling the story.

Now, let me share with you what happened back then.

Part Two
Middle

4.

THE NIGHT HAD COME on faster than David would've liked.

*

Is this story about me?

How 'bout you listen to the rest of it before you decide? Yeah?

Sounds like a plan.

God, you're so fucking smug, sitting over there, judging me instead of getting to know and understand me. Lord, the things I'd love to do to you. Look at you. LOOK AT YOU! Fuck. I'm getting hard as a rock just thinking about what I could do to you if you'd just whisper 'please.'

Can I continue? Or are you going to keep interrupting me with your shit questions?

Good.

*

Aided by only the shining stars and his trusty shofar, a goat horn to ward off evil, tucked between his leather belt and his body, David followed the path.

'A man needs to follow the path,' the priest would say during their daily teachings. 'A man that strays from the path will find misfortunate and illness.'

Nary an animal hooted or hollered.

David was unnerved, but still he walked on. He continued through the trees, aware this rite of passage was what separated him from achieving all that his Faith wanted for him. Failure would send him cascading into the Abyss, and an eternity of searching would await.

To a man, this was no easy journey. It was the culmination of years of dedicated service under the guidance of the trusted, and being watched over through the eyes of the Lord.

"For I am righteous, and I am pure, and my God protects me," he said, clutching the Shofar tightly. If he was confronted, the goat horn would act as a deterrent.

The path that each prospective graduate needed to walk led from their school, which was nothing but a quaint cabin, along the river's edge, before it veered through the trees and ultimately looped around back to the school.

There was no time limit to complete it.

To be successful, each student was required to walk the path at night, alone. When they returned, three instructors would question them on what they experienced, and determine if they'd remained on the path before them or whether evil had somehow slipped in.

David had stood with Father Selinofoto, an older man whom he admired greatly. Even with the arthritic changes in the man's hands, David held onto him until the school bell sounded and Father Selinofoto nodded.

"David, my son. Before you go, know this. What awaits you is not what you expect. A trickster will do whatever it takes to gain an inch before taking a mile."

David nodded. He kissed the back of the man's hand, and set off.

At first, he was confident.

He'd walked this path a thousand times before. Once before morning prayer, once after lunch, every day over the course of the decade he'd been at the school. Not to mention the times they simply went for a stroll, enjoying the quietness of nature and the direct access to their Lord above in the stillness.

But never once had he walked this path at night. If he was to spend time outside once dark, he'd join some of the other students near the school, who'd all take a place on the grass and peacefully watch the stars above.

How he'd loved those evenings. He relied on his familiarity of the pathway and the security in his beliefs as he approached the river. Nothing awaited him, which strengthened his resolve to continue and accept that he would be successful.

"For I am righteous, and I am pure, and my God protects me," he repeated, even as the trees appeared to crowd the edges of the path and the canopy of branches blocked almost all of the moon's illumination.

"FOR I AM RIGHTEOUS!"

He yelled it unprompted. David had the overwhelming sensation he was being watched, that something had snuck up on him and was moving closer.

He continued walking, not allowing himself to become frozen by fear. He knew he should be reciting scripture, appealing to the heavenly divine to remain by his side, but his fear was such that he was unable to remember any of it. Shame flushed his face. If Father Selinofoto learned of this transgression, David knew he'd be sent for one hundred lashes.

With the river no longer visible behind him, he began to hum to himself, a tune they often sang while kicking an old ball during their free time. It was the only way for him to push down the growing fear that he was absolutely being watched. A branch cracked nearby, his pulse quickening.

For I am a son of God. For I am protected by my Faith.

He began to repeat this over and over in his head, which resulted in him humming the mantra.

David stopped when he came to understand whatever was watching him was humming the tune along with him.

The air had never been this cold, he knew, so he forced himself forward, continuing to hum, gripping the shofar harder. The horn would not break, not from his hand wrapped around it, but a tiny part of his mind wondered what would happen if it did. He'd be left defenseless if the evil should arise.

A sound.

Buzzing.

From further ahead.

It made him question what he had gotten himself into. He'd made sure not to listen to any of the students who went the nights previous, as he knew they'd either create some elaborate story in an attempt to scare the others, or they'd not speak of anything, either too afraid to share, or simply because nothing happened.

But in the bits and pieces that David had overheard, no one had mentioned another person, or a buzzing.

There was just enough light for him to see an object ahead. It was the source of the buzzing, and as he approached, the dark mass of flies grew louder. There must've been thousands of them. A stench overcame him as he leaned in. He used his forearm to cover his nose, but even then, his thick robe couldn't block out the overwhelming smell that came from the object.

Against his better judgement, he kicked at it, his foot scattering the flies from the mass. It was a sloppy, solid thing, whatever it was. When he made contact, it squelched, and he heard a liquid movement that made his guts boil.

As though a rope were attached from the mass to David's midsection, he felt himself pulled forward, dropping to his knees. Now, so close to the lump of putrefaction, he could see what it was. He shouldn't have been able to, considering how dark it was, but something let his eyes adjust and when it came into horrifying detail, he couldn't stop the bile from spewing forth from between his fingers, fingers that attempted to keep his mouth shut and prevent the scream from escaping.

It was Father Selinofoto's head.

The face had been shredded, but even with the jagged slashes, David recognized who it belonged to easily enough. The edges of the neck were grotesque, as though several predators had taken turns gnawing it free from his body. This, of course, was impossible, David tried to tell himself, for he'd been talking to Father Selinofoto before the test began. Maggots began to crawl from the dark wounds, the flies returning to feed and lay their infernal eggs. David stood, bent at the waist, and vomited again. Straightening, he wiped his mouth clean with the back of his forearm.

"Awful."

That single word, spoken from so close behind, and from a voice he didn't recognize, caused David to let out a squeal. It was a noise he wasn't proud of, but the fright had been so severe he simply couldn't prevent it.

He stumbled away, jumping over the buzzing flies, and fell onto the dirt path, the shofar bouncing free and disappearing into the darkened night.

"You won't need that, David. It wouldn't have done you any good anyways."

The figure who'd spoken so near to him stepped closer. David's mouth fell open when he saw it was Father Selinofoto. *It can't be.* He gazed at the buzzing mass in horror, before looking again at the figure standing there. The harder he stared, the more he realized it wasn't him, but a vision of the man, a pretend version. It was as though even the shadows actively worked to blur any details from David.

"Who're you?" David asked, getting shakily to his feet. Even if this man said the shofar would be of no use, he'd found a comforting security in having it in his possession.

The figure moved around the decaying mass on the path, and it was in that sidestep that the Father's robe parted just enough that David saw its legs were not human, and that its feet were that of what should adorn a clawed beast. The air around him rapidly dropped in temperature, so much so that thick, white clouds puffed out in front of him as he breathed.

"Who I *am* doesn't matter, little one. I'm here to show you what's *there*," the figure said, pointing above them with an outstretched hand. The night disguised enough of the figure's features, but David could see that its fingers were wretched things, and that the hair that covered its arm was thick and dark. What lay under that robe was something David hoped he'd never find out.

When he looked Father Selinofoto in the eyes again, he saw an evil burning deep within the pupils, an evil that caressed some part of his subconscious, begging him to open up, to accept this evil into his soul and let it live there forever.

"BACK FOULNESS!" he yelled, finding the nerve to step away from the figure and put some distance between them.

The figure let out a harsh laugh akin to a rabid dog's bark, and shook its head.

"Your false words of faith won't deter what it is I want from you. You think begging someone who doesn't know who you are will keep you safe? I'm right here. I know who you are. I'm here David. Let me in, son."

David turned and ran.

He didn't know if this was part of the test, or an elaborate joke being played on him by the other students, but he no longer cared. He needed to get out of these trees and off this path immediately. His heart was pounding in his chest as he ran, but no matter how hard he pushed himself, he could hear the figure right behind him. Glancing back, his eyes went wide as he saw the figure bounding after him on all fours, as though it had transformed into more of a beast than a man during its pursuit.

I'm not going to make it, David thought, as the figure got so close, he could feel its claws connecting with the backs of his shoes. *Lord above, I beg you, please come to me in my time of need.*

"The one you pray to isn't listening, but the one that's right behind you will grant you your wish."

David darted to his right and kicked a root, stumbling, but he was confident he'd managed to elude the figure, allowing him enough time to turn and confront this *thing* with the cross that resided on a loop of rope around his neck.

"BACK!"

He yelled at the figure at the top of his lungs, holding the cross out in front of him as far as he could, which wasn't far considering the length of rope.

"A cross? A cross doesn't stop me!" The figure laughed. "You have a cross, but I got a fucking rope," it said, suddenly lashing out at David. A length of rope flew over his head and wrapped around his neck. He let go of the cross, letting it drop to his chest as he struggled to pull the rope free. The beast yanked as hard as it could, pulling David towards it. As David stumbled and fell, the figure extended its hand and the sharp claws sank into David's chest. He let out a howl of agony as his skin was pierced and his insides sliced open.

"Nunc es mei..." the figure whispered, still holding him up by the noose around his neck.

Now, you are mine.

5.

RACHEL ENTERED THE BOARDROOM suddenly feeling like she was in the hot seat. Sure, she'd asked Carl Bagg, Head of the Institution, to organize this meeting, but when she walked in and saw the six men already sitting there, looking at her, she wanted to turn around and flee. That had been an internal fear mechanism she'd identified when she was in high school. She'd taken some adult oriented after school courses to help, as well as a public speaking course, which had aided her greatly, especially with the rampant sexism she'd dealt with when she'd graduated high school early and had challenged the final three years of her degree. When she'd completed her certification and became an official board-certified Psychologist at twenty-three, she'd had to stand up for herself repeatedly, and her early identification of her own internal shortcomings had been instrumental in granting her the strength needed to succeed. Especially when a majority of her colleagues were twice her age.

"Gentlemen," she said, nodding and taking her seat.

"I'm officially bringing this meeting to order," said Carl. "Sheryl, thank you for your diligent note taking. Has everyone read the transcription from the last meeting, dated..." Carl flipped through the papers he had before him, stopping when he spotted the date, "November twenty-first?"

Everybody replied that they had, which put Rachel at ease. She'd become accustomed to the senior members coming unprepared to meetings requested by younger females.

"Let's cut to the chase," said Carl. "Darryl, you've gone over the video footage and the accompanying notes. Patient David – and I reiterate that we have his last name as Stewart, but that he denies it is his real last name – has continued to show regression. We need to come up with a clear plan to treat him." Carl crossed his hands on the boardroom table. "Darryl, what is your professional opinion regarding this, now that you're up to speed?"

Beside Rachel, Dr. Darryl Dravendash leaned back in his chair, putting both hands behind his head, and looked around the room at each of them. She was unsure if he was trying to be dramatic or needed a second to compose himself, but either way, the posturing created an unexpected ripple of annoyance to course through her. Darryl was close to Rachel in age, just seven years older, and had spent his life investigating what he referred to as religious reactions, or what happens when people go too far in their beliefs. His masters in theology had been something he'd presented on around the globe, and even though he was currently annoying her, she had always been thrilled to have him as a colleague. He was someone she could bounce ideas off and have it approached from several different angles.

"I've never seen anything like this. I've spent my life researching and studying the academia aspect of Religion, the Bible and the people and events within. Of course, when looking at David's behavior as a whole... I must confess, it looks to me as though he's putting on a big show. How many hours a day does he read the Bible?"

"He's never had access to the Bible here," Harvey replied.

"Seriously? From what I've heard him say on the tapes, and some of the Latin he's used, I would've expected him to be reading three or four different Bibles at least ten hours a day, if not more."

"You said 'when looking at David's behavior as a whole.' What does that mean, precisely?" Wilson asked, pushing past Darryl's enthusiastic estimation.

"What I mean is, when I take the totality of his performance, from the first interview when he arrived, to the one of him telling the story of the religious student meeting a demon in the woods, it is a convincing portrayal of a man with multiple personalities who is trying to control his own narrative. But..." Darryl said, fading off and holding up his hands.

"But what?" Carl replied.

"But, if I pull out a few *very* specific moments of video footage, and was only shown those specific moments, I'd be led to believe we were dealing with an actual case of possession."

A chuckle came from near Rachel. She looked over at the elderly priest dressed in full formal cassock. She found it ridiculous that the man was wearing what he would wear to deliver his weekly sermon, but she assumed it was possibly one way for him to get free coffee and prime parking spots.

"Pffft, come off it, Dravendash," Father Gio said, a sarcastic smirk plastered on his face as he looked directly at Darryl. "Surely you can't be serious?"

"One hundred percent," Darryl replied.

"I'm hard pressed to believe that, within the walls of this facility we currently sit in, there is a man who is *actually* possessed. Do you hear yourself?" Father Gio shook his head in disbelief. Rachel looked at Carl, the man raising his eyebrows when they met eyes, but she wasn't sure if that meant he also couldn't believe it, or that he was surprised Father Gio was questioning it.

"Do *you* hear yourself?" Darryl replied.

"Oh, come off it," Father Gio said. Darryl and Father Gio began to bicker back and forth, the volume rising quickly, and soon enough the two of them were on their feet, hurling insults back and forth.

"Sheesh, look at the men getting all worked up. So emotional," Rachel said, trying to defuse the situation. She had to admit, it was the politest argument she might've ever witnessed, neither man uttering a single profanity.

Rachel waited until the two had returned to their seats before jumping in.

"Father Gio, you're painting a far different picture of this patient than when we met previously, just the two of us," Rachel said.

"I've had time to gather my thoughts. Make more prudent and rational observations."

Rachel took him in for a moment, seeing the return of the smugness that seemed to have been tattooed on the man's face. His glasses had slipped lower on his whiskey-reddened nose, but he'd yet to make the effort to push them back up.

"Look, I've been working with David since he arrived. Over that time, I've been unable to connect with him or have him open up in any meaningful way. The only way I've been able to communicate with him is to allow him to lead, and direct him from there. He's an interesting case. I can't substantiate anything that Dravendash may profess regarding 'possession,' but I can say that there have been times David has expressed various things that he shouldn't have any knowledge of." Rachel had hoped that she wouldn't have to discuss this but seeing how easily off the tracks this meeting had gone, and would go again if some direction wasn't implemented, she knew she needed to share.

"Such as?" Carl asked, one hand now supporting his head, as though he was fighting off sleep.

"I'm not sure I feel comfortable sharing those details in this environment, sir."

"We're all professionals here, Rachel. If it has to do with this particular patient's care and treatment, I think we should hear it."

Rachel noticed Carl look towards her. She could see his expression change, one showing that he immediately regretted forcing her to share what she was about to share. She knew she could request to speak with him privately after, but instead she nodded and spoke.

"The patient was able to describe in detail a sexual assault I experienced when I was sixteen. I never reported this assault, as it occurred at a high school party. The individual who assaulted me, a classmate, was killed in a drunk driving accident approximately two hours after the assault. The patient should not have any information regarding this incident."

"Jesus, I'm so sorry, Rachel," Dr. Victor Hamesl said. It was the first time he'd spoken since the meeting started, which was often the case. He was an observer by nature, a man of few words. He often conveyed his thoughts to her with changes in his face; a smile here, a frown there, an adjustment of his spectacles after hearing something he disagreed with. He'd always been one of her staunchest supporters, no matter the thirty-year age difference between the two.

"Thank you, Victor."

"I ask this with the utmost respect, but something you said suggests I ask. Was there anything else the patient knew that he shouldn't have?" Carl asked, his entire body showing just how uncomfortable he was with having made Rachel share this.

"Yes," she replied, clearing her throat.

"Would you share that as well? If not, we can discuss that later. Privately."

"As a result of that sexual assault, I discovered that I was pregnant. My parents wouldn't allow me to have it, and so I had an abortion. The patient also knew this. He was able to tell me on what day I had it, who the doctor was that performed the procedure, and even what I secretly would've named the baby, had I carried it to term."

Rachel had never shared any of that with any of her colleagues, and had never once shared with another person that she would've named her unborn child George if it had been a boy, and Laurel if it had been a girl.

"Rachel, I am so very sorry. This is also unbelievable. Do we have him saying this on film?" Hamesl said, sitting up straighter and reaching over to squeeze Rachel's forearm. It was an act Rachel cherished deeply, and she was thankful he'd done it.

"Not on video, but it was recorded on the normal audio recording system that is in each interview room and can be easily recovered," she said.

"Doctor Hoggendorf, I am very sorry to hear your news. My sincere apologies that one of God's children did such a vile act," Father Anderson said. Rachel had only spoken to him briefly before on the phone, asking him specific questions regarding things David had said. Even over the phone he seemed like a pompous asshole, and having met him in person, she felt that even more.

"Please, Father. I don't believe in a higher power; I'd rather not hear useless words regarding an act that happened to me."

"I apologize," he said, which Rachel replied to with a nod.

"Once again," Dravendash said, shaking his head while looking at some of the notes, "I state, taken as a whole this patient presents as a highly probable schizophrenic adult male, or at least a male suffering from bipolar disorder with multiple personalities. BUT. Some of these individual aspects have kept me up at night."

Father Gio scoffed at Dravendash, shaking his head for a very different reason. The priest's face looked like it might explode, his cheeks puffing in and out and his eyes narrowed.

"I struggle to accept what you are saying, Doctor. I've known you for, what? Almost a decade? You've spoken at a number of conferences that I've attended and some that we've even shared panels on, but this is the first where I've honestly questioned what it is you're saying here. You believe he is possessed?" Father Gio finished and looked at the others, his expression going from sheer anger to now hoping that one of the others would chuckle, show that they also thought Dravendash was off his rocker.

"Do you believe in possession?" Dravendash countered.

"Well, I mean it's hardly –"

"Yes or no. Do you believe in possession?"

"What? Am I the patient here all of a sudden?"

Rachel found she was enjoying Father Gio squirming under Dravendash's questions and firm gaze.

"Have you watched any of the particular footage of David?" Dravendash asked.

"No," Father Gio replied, with a tone in his voice bordering on defeat.

"Can we get that footage in here? I think it would be beneficial for us, and Father Gio most of all, to see what it is I'm suggesting."

6.

RACHEL HATED THE INTAKE room. It was too small, leaving the attending doctor vulnerable if an unexpected outburst were to happen. Even with the patient restrained, it didn't negate the fact they were practically sitting on each other's laps.

The room had a wooden table in the middle. As needed, chairs were brought in, pre-determined by who needed to be in attendance. Sometimes it was simply the patient and doctor. Other times, a court-ordered individual would also be present, other times a lawyer or, in rare cases, a family member. Double-sided mirrors adorned the walls on either side of the table. The single entrance was a door that opened via a buzzer system.

On that day, Rachel was seated in one of the chairs, an 8x11 notepad flipped open on the table in front of her. She held a patient file, and rhythmically tapped her pen against the paper as she re-read the details.

A buzz sounded, prompting her to look in the direction of the door.

It opened, and two guards escorted a sheepish looking male in. His wrists were cuffed, and the guards pulled him along by his arms. He was able to wipe his long brown hair from his eyes, as well as blow it away with upturned lips. The guards forced him into the chair directly across from Dr. Hoggendorf and proceeded to affix the patient's cuffs to the metal loop that protruded from the tabletop.

Once they had him secured, the two guards moved to the back of the room, leaning against the mirrored wall.

"You two can leave us, it's ok," Rachel said to the guards.

"Nah, sorry Doc, after his behavior this morning, Wilson's asked us to stay," the taller guard said. Rachel couldn't remember his name. She'd dealt with him before, but for some reason she never remembered if his name was Larry or Terry.

"No problem," she replied, turning her head to the patient and smiling. David's head was down, his hair covering his eyes.

"We'll need to arrange for a haircut. That looks awfully annoying. And have they given you new clothes? Since you ripped up the other ones?"

David nodded; face still downturned.

"Today can go one of two ways, David. This can be a quick visit and we'll get you off to your room. We'll get you showered and off to lunch. Or, if you're not going to be forthcoming with me, this can take all day. It's really up to you. I'm here to help," she said, fighting the urge to lean forward and touch his forearm. She'd struggled to make any headway with him, any connection at all. In all their interviews, she'd frequently gotten to the point where she'd have happily bashed her head off the wall in frustration rather than sit and stare at him, waiting for a response that never came.

She brought her attention back to him, watching as he slumped in the chair across from her and sure that, no matter how brilliant her peers thought she was, she'd never find a way to bridge the gap between her and him.

"I've reviewed your file again, David. I have to say, it seems like you've had a pretty rough time so far. Would you like to discuss this, or shall we postpone a deeper dive into your background until our session tomorrow?" It was almost a shot in the dark, a way for her to put the ball back in his court and make him decide how the session was going to go. To her surprise, he looked up and spoke.

"My name is David. I am almost four hundred years old. Nobody ever believes me, but it is the truth. I was once a student. Now... I just want this pain to stop."

David began to weep. At first it was quiet, his head down again. Rachel leaned in slightly to try and see if he was alright, before his weeping grew to full-on deep sobbing, his shoulders moving up and down with each one.

"It hurts so bad. I don't want this. Please, please take this pain away. I never asked to walk down this path!"

David screamed and thrashed. At first both guards leaned forward, watching to see what he was going to do, but when he raised his head as though ready to slam his face into the table, they rushed over, grabbing him by the shoulders and holding him in the chair. Rachel wanted them to be gentle and to not escalate the situation, but she understood that, for David's safety and theirs, they needed to hold him tight. As he attempted to thrash, Rachel clapped loudly, getting his eyes to focus on her for the briefest of seconds. It was all the opening she needed.

"David, that's why you're here. We want to help you. *I* want to help you," she said, smiling at him.

"You can't help me, you clueless bitch!"

He thrashed again, the table jolting. The guards pushed him forward, slamming his head onto the table. Rachel pushed back on her chair. The sudden outburst was something she should've expected, yet still it startled her.

"Nobody ever believes me!" David ranted. "Nobody can ever help! TAKE IT OUT."

His body visibly sagged, allowing him to slip forward out of the chair, which toppled backwards behind him. His knees hit the floor hard with a dense *whack* as the two guards adjusted their hold on him so the cuffs didn't rip his hands off.

"We're done," Rachel said. "Please, take him to his room. We'll resume tomorrow."

David let out a groan, rigidity returning to his body only after the guards unclipped him from the metal loop. His back arched, his legs planting beneath him. The guards sensed it, leaned into him, and grabbed him tightly around each arm.

"Please, let me go. Please. I can't stay here. You won't believe me. No one ever does!"

To Rachel's surprise, he made a sound like that of an angry pig, a deep, guttural squeal before pushing upwards against both guards, toppling them backwards. They stumbled, colliding with the mirrors. Rachel immediately pushed the panic button that was clipped to her jacket pocket. David smiled, his eyes wider, longer, as though that of a predatory animal, not a medicated man.

And then it happened. For the briefest of moments, David's ears elongated. Rachel saw it, and when David noticed her shock, he smiled wider, and then the illusion was gone. She knew it shouldn't have come as a surprise – she practically expected to see his teeth transforming into sharp canine teeth, but as his lips pulled back, the two guards tackled him, their collective weight enough to push him to the floor.

The door opened, three more guards rushing in, surveying the room briefly before aiding their two colleagues in subduing the patient and getting him back to his feet.

Rachel and David locked eyes as he was led out, and for a moment she knew someone else – no *something* else – was looking at her from behind his eyes.

Then he blinked, and the tired, frightened, feeble patient returned.

*

Dravendash watched Father Gio's face for the entirety of the viewing of the interview footage, while Rachel and Darryl waited for the exact moment when David's shift occurred, his body seemingly changing and becoming something else for a split second before returning to normal. When the footage ended, Darryl raised his eyebrows at Gio, as if to say, 'So, what do you think now?'

Father Gio cleared his throat but refused to look at anybody else.

"Maybe we adjourn this meeting and reconnect after we each have some time to digest what we've discussed, and what was on that tape," Harvey said.

"Works for me," Carl replied, faster than Rachel appreciated. Before she was able to say another word, the room emptied, and she was left alone at the table.

7.

I᙭ ʜᴀᴅ ᴋᴇᴘᴛ Rᴀᴄʜᴇʟ up far later than she would've liked.

No matter what she did, her mind kept pulling her back to David, and how his face seemed to transform. The same thoughts had tormented her the day of the interview, but after having reviewed the tape while Father Gio watched it, the fear had come back full-force, and it was as though she simply could not disconnect from it.

When she finally fell asleep, she had horrible dreams, nightmares involving strange beasts with elongated tentacles that writhed and undulated, the suckers grabbing her legs and pulling her, kicking and screaming, towards a group of people who begged for whatever hideousness that was happening to them to stop.

*

Rachel was sitting in her chair when two guards escorted David into the formal interview room. It was larger than the intake room, a place designed for longer, more in-depth conversations, with a couch for the patient and a matching chair for the interviewer to sit in. The room was predominantly light grey, with some softer brown accent colors and pieces. The guards stopped in front of the couch, where David's wrist cuffs were removed. His ankle cuffs remained, which caused him to stumble and drop onto the couch.

Unable to right himself, he struggled into a sitting position. Recalling the previous outburst, Rachel didn't move, instead allowing the guards to help him. Once he was upright, they backed away, remaining just out of sight.

Rachel decided to wait for David to get comfortable. He shifted and squirmed before he let out an audible sigh.

"Hello, David."

At the sound of Rachel's voice, he raised his head, as though he'd only now realized she was in the room. As he flipped his hair from his eyes, Rachel focused on his face, wondering if she would see another change. But it wasn't his structure that subtly altered. It was his voice.

"I need to talk to my mom. Can you call her? She'll be worried sick."

The voice was not that of David's. At least not the same one from the previous interview.

Rachel reacted with surprise, shifting her weight in the chair.

"David, do you know who your mother is? Your file indicates that you were found as a child on the doorstep of the St. Vincent Catholic Church. To my knowledge, you were five years old."

David began rapidly shaking his head, his hands clenched together so tightly that his fingers went white.

"No. That's not right. No, no, no, no, no. I went for a walk. Mommy said I could go for a walk. She said I could, so I did. I didn't talk to no one."

"David," Rachel said, shifting closer to him as she gently placed her hand on his leg. She knew this wasn't something she should be doing, but at that moment she had no idea how to get through to him. When her hand made contact, he visibly lurched, an act so unexpected and violent that Rachel screamed and leaped backwards, hitting the arm of the chair and flipping over it onto the ground. The guards rushed forward, one going to help Rachel, who waved him off as she stood, and the other going to David, who sat completely still.

"It's okay. Thank you, both of you, but it's okay," Rachel said as she returned to the chair. She focused on David. "Do you know where you are?"

He turned to her when she spoke his name. For an unflinching thirty seconds, he stared without blinking.

"I'm somewhere I shouldn't be," he finally said, his voice returning to what Rachel recognized as David's. *Or is it?* She knew how far schizophrenic people with multiple personalities could go when it came to portraying each of their identities. Maybe the David she first met wasn't the real David, his 'true' identity?

"And why is that?"

"Because it came to me, *into me*, and it won't go away. All I ever wanted was to learn and be a good human and it took it all away."

David began to cry again; Rachel pulled a tissue from a box on the side table and handed it to him. He took it, holding the tissue in his hands for a moment before dabbing his eyes.

"I wish it would've killed me in that forest. So much pain would've been prevented."

The words came out in an almost imperceptible whisper, but Rachel heard them.

"What forest?"

"From my test," he replied. "To graduate."

Rachel flipped through his file, pausing in a few places before moving on.

"David, I'm sorry, you've lost me. I see nothing about prior cognitive tests here, or even anything to suggest you were ever in public school."

"There wouldn't be. Too many years ago. And I wasn't found as a child outside that church. That's just the cover story. Father Burke kept me hidden. He knew what I was. If you don't believe me, ask him."

"You know we can't do that," Rachel said, tapping her pen against the file folder.

"And why's that?" David replied with a level of anger. Rachel looked at him with the expectation that he was about to attack her. To her relief she found him still sitting, but his jaw was clenched, the muscles near his ears flexing.

"David, I know you think you're smarter than every physician here, but I can guarantee you, we've seen it all before. I may look younger than the other doctors you've met, but trust me when I say, you can't fool me."

"I know what happened to you," David quietly said.

As he said that, Rachel gasped, the front of David's grey sweatpants soaking through with urine as he pissed himself.

"David. I expect some level of patient professionalism, especially if your desire is to leave this place."

"Don't lie to me."

His reply was blunt, and, even with a darkened crotch, he looked as though he was on the edge of lashing out.

Rachel sat further back, the two staring at each other.

"Why did you kill Father Burke?"

She asked the question in a calm, easy tone, but David's response was anything but.

"I didn't kill that piece of shit! He was a child molester! A rapist! He did unthinkable things to young and old, all under the guise of faith and redemption! He deserved what he got! He deserved it!"

David stood rapidly, his ankle cuffs causing him to stumble forward, losing his balance. Unable to stop himself, he crashed to the floor face first. Rachel had sprung from her chair in an attempt to grab him, but she was too slow. Both guards raced over, pulling him to his knees, and as they did so, David's right hand darted out. The guard nearest him let out a gurgled cry and fell, clutching at his neck. Blood was already pumping from his destroyed jugular, his hands unable to staunch the flow. The second guard pushed David back to the floor, yanking both of his hands behind his back and slapping cuffs on him. While doing this, he radioed for backup and medical. Once that was done, he went to the injured guard, but it was too late. The man lay half on the couch, half on the floor, his hands still wrapped around his neck but no longer capable of applying any pressure. The wound was fatal.

Alarms blared as six others hustled into the room. A male went to check on Rachel, while three went to the deceased and two to the guard and David. As David was escorted from the room, he looked to the camera and smiled, giving it a wink just before disappearing from view.

8.

I'VE NEVER SPOKEN OF Father Burke to anyone.

Yes, yes. I told Rachel about him and so what? So. Fucking. What. What're you going to do about it?

NOTHING.

Fucking HELL. Oh, you find that funny?

Tee-Hee.

No, I'm not actually laughing. Would you laugh if what you wanted was taken away? What if what you were told would happen never did? Do you remember the sacred scripture? The words spoken in the necessary manner. What about the ritual, hmmm? The one that we all followed... and what happened?

Nothing, with a capital fucking N.

I made a pact with the dark. I swore an oath to what would await me, and what has it gotten me?

Imprisonment.

You don't think I'm imprisoned? Think about it.

I ended up here, IN HERE, and for what? A body useless to me, useless for what I need to do, need to accomplish.

Burke had it coming. I didn't do what I did to save David. Far from it. But Burke got what he deserved.

Sinners and liars always do.

9.

Email correspondence between Chief of Staff, Harvey Wilson and Head of Institution, Carl Bagg, following the death of guard, Nigel McConnell.

Emails and date/time redacted.

From Harvey Wilson to Carl Bagg

Carl, what happened here? Have you watched the footage? We need answers immediately. If the press gets a hold of this story and we don't have answers, we're both out of a job.

From Carl Bagg to Harvey Wilson (reply sent approx. twenty minutes later)

Harvey, I've watched the footage. I would suggest you do as well. I've called a press conference for tomorrow morning at nine a.m. sharp. I'll be calling McConnell's wife shortly to let her know, and to offer our condolences. I'll draft up a standard payout statement for her and I will also be giving her the life insurance information for her to collect. Because of this patient's 'newness' to us, I've authorized the inclusion of the extra two-hundred-and fifty-thousand-dollars for accidental death occurrence. I think it's a fair thing to do. I know normally we need to vote on this, but I'm overriding that.

I want Dr. Hoggendorf to continue working with this patient, but I think we also need to review safety protocols going forward and I'd like Dr. Dravendash to be brought in for some sessions. Please review this with Dr. Hoggendorf and schedule accordingly.

From Harvey Wilson to Carl Bagg (reply sent approx. sixty minutes later)

Mother of God, Carl. What did I just watch? I've instructed Rachel and Darryl to watch it as well. We need to keep them at a distance while working with that patient. In fact, I suggest we either have him cuffed at all times, or in a straight jacket. Whatever happened with his hand, whatever that was that the slow-mo shows, it can't be real, can it?

From Carl Bagg to Harvey Wilson (reply sent approx. two minutes later)

Nigel's wife has retained a lawyer. We must do what we can to not allow that tape to be released to his team or to the public. I've made a backup copy but will have the techs delete the ending.

It must *never* be allowed to be seen by anyone else.

From Dr. Rachel Hoggendorf to Carl Bagg, Dr. Darryl Dravendash and Harvey Wilson (email sent approx. ninety minutes later)

Gentlemen, I've watched the tape several times. I'm unable to offer up any sort of scientific explanation as to what happened. I know I've heard conjecture regarding his hand transforming into some 'beast-like' claw, but I was in the room, and I saw nothing of the sort. Nor, as a medical doctor and a pragmatic individual, can I give that notion any credence. I'd like to continue on with the patient, but with the necessary security concerns implemented. If needed, we can conduct our interviews with plexiglass between us, as was done in the past with dangerous patients. I'm also in agreement that I think it would benefit David substantially if Dr. Dravendash comes on board. I think having some sessions with both of us present and some with just myself or Darryl would be tolerable to David, while also allowing progress to be made.

From Dr. Darryl Dravendash to Dr. Rachel Hoggendorf, Carl Bagg and Harvey Wilson (reply sent approx. ten minutes later)

I've not been able to see the footage, but at this point, I don't think it's necessary. I'd not want to pollute my view of this patient based on potential pixilation that may or may not have my brain see something that might not be there. I'll sit in with Rachel's next session, and we can create a schedule going forward.

10.

What happened after that night?

So much. Nothing at all.

Cliché? Maybe.

But it's the truth.

I was a slave to both sides. A man stuck barking at the moon for reprieve. A creature forever trapped in this mortal bag of bones. I've done all I could, taken my desires as far as they could go. But then it got me thinking.

Hmmmm. Yes. Yes!

It was when I was travelling through the streets of Rome that I met another travelling man, one who shared similar traits to myself, if you get my drift.

Oh, how we danced and loved and dined on the sins of those who dared yell at us in the alleys at night.

I've never felt feelings for anyone else like I did for him.

His name?

Not important.

Yes, yes, I understand, you're sitting there right now, taking your notes, and trying to figure out if I'm telling the truth and if I am who I say I am.

At first, he asked me to call him Utu, a man whom I trusted dearly and one who sated my needs above and below the sheets. Oh, don't look so stunned. Look at the crimes the Christians perpetrate on so many. You don't think those who serve the devil like to suck dick? Utu was my sun and my moon. But that all changed when he revealed that he'd taken that character upon himself to protect me from who he really was.

That, I will not tell you.

But some called him the Angel of the Abyss. Do what you will with that. He told me all about the black heavens and the land of ash and...

I'm sorry. I'm getting off topic.

Yes, I'm aroused. No, I won't piss myself again.

So unfortunate what happened to that guard.

So unnecessary.

Or was it?

Maybe that was something I needed to do to bring me closer to leaving this wretched hole behind.

You take all the notes you want; you jot them down with your pretty little fingers and your lips that beg to devour what lies between my legs.

In due time.

I'll eat every morsel of you when the time to devour is upon us.

*

My father did what he could. Always and forever.

I dreamed a dream of him once. Would you like to hear about it?

*

The sky was red in all directions. I remember that the most.

I awoke on a mountain top, the land below a mix of greens and blues. Lush vegetation and water surrounded it. I'd never seen a more glorious place. It was paradise.

A bellow from the base of where I woke sounded, an animal I'd never heard before. Was it a beast or simply one of 'God's' creatures? I needed to find out.

As I began my journey down, I understood that I was a child, maybe ten years old. I felt emboldened for some reason, as though nothing could hurt me and nothing would want to.

Why would anything want to hurt me, I remember thinking. Just then a rabbit came bounding along, joining me in my hike to find out what had bellowed.

'Hello, Mr. Rabbit,' I said, watching as its nose wiggled and its tail wagged as it hopped along. Something joined me on my other side, and, looking over, I saw it to be a long-horned goat.

'Hello, Mr. Goat,' I said, the smile on my face the largest it had ever been.

A hissing, slithering sound occurred, and above me in the tree, I saw a long, thick snake dangling from a branch.

'Hello, Mr. Snake,' I said, as it dropped from the treetop and swallowed the rabbit. 'Good, best to not be hungry,' I told it, once it had swallowed the rabbit whole. It took the rabbit's place and slithered along beside me. Seeing a dense bush, I went to it and filled my hands with feed. Returning, I let my friend, the goat, eat up, laughing as its tongue and lips tickled my hands. 'Good, best to have your energy,' I told it, once it had licked all of the grains free from my palms.

Soon, we arrived at the bottom of the path, three directions splitting off from the main trail.

'You go left, you go right, I'll take the middle,' I told my friends, knowing I'd see them again and that we'd never return the same as we were.

As so often is the case, we said our goodbyes, shedding a tear for our separation. I, on the one hand, had enjoyed my brief time spent with my two companions, but I was ready to discover what lay in wait.

I don't know what my friends encountered, but my path was a simple, flat trail through the trees, worn into being through the passing of thousands of others. It was as though I was connecting with those who'd taken this journey before me, those who'd dreamed this dream and discovered what I was about to discover. How long did I walk? As long as one walks in a dream, as long as it took for me to arrive at the statue.

A stone statue greeted me as I entered a clearing, and I heard the stars go out in the sky, one by one. It was an unsettling and cathartic experience; click, click, click. The sky above went black, the stone illuminating in a grey hue that allowed me to see the figure that had been carved into the hard material.

It was my two friends, goat and snake, entangled and hybrid, making one creature, a being that I immediately bowed down before. It was only then that I noticed my hands were trembling. Was it from excitement? Fear? Both. For I knew that I'd walked the path towards this destination with the two who were the statue, who'd guided me here. But it was also then I understood that I stared upon the true vision of my father, and that I had fed him and conversed with him and done right within his mind.

A bellow.

A summoning.

Was it by beast or by horn?

From where I knelt, I was unable to discern what had created the sound, but either way it called, and I answered.

Oh, my mighty liege, accept thy fealty to thou forever.

Did I think that or speak it aloud?

I was unknowing as I left the statue and continued. If I'd stayed, I would've seen how the darkest of blood began to leak from the eyes and pour from the mouths.

With my shoulders back and my head held high, I continued.

Do you know that moment when it gets dark, and you look upon the stars in the sky and you understand that each little light above is forever? That each shining beacon is where you could be, where you should be, and at that exact second, you could be whomever and wherever you longed to be?

I was cursed. Cursed to be walking away from the vision of my father under stars that wouldn't call to me and let me answer.

A bellow.

By horn.

This time I was certain. I picked up my pace, moving towards the source with an unhinged excitement and an unquenched fury. Saliva dripped from my mouth, forcing me to wipe my face with my forearm even as I wanted to suck it back in and savor the taste.

I had a sense that I was nearing my destination. This was confirmed when I saw the fires burning along the path, guiding me to where I needed to be. Some search their entire lives looking for that place, but here I was, beckoned to it. How lucky, wouldn't you say?

Stepping into a space surrounded by statues of those who've ruled the cosmos, I initially felt disappointment, finding the statue of my father residing in the middle. Why was it here again? That thought was pushed from my mind when I saw the snake's eyes blink and its tongue dart. The goat bleated.

I knelt, and the statue crumbled, revealing my Father in all his otherworldly glory.

*

I awoke then.

At first, I was angry, Dr. Dravendash. Uh-huh, I was. Wouldn't you be? Not you, no never you. That one there. The ones watching us from above. Can you see them, Dr. Hoggendorf? You mean there are two of you *professionals* here and neither of you can see whom I speak of?

What happened after I woke up?

I knew who'd prevented me from ever seeing my father, from reuniting with the one who'd left me those letters.

Yes, that's right. I went to him. Took care of the sinner.

Took care of the liar.

11.

AFTER THE SESSION ENDED, Rachel and Darryl met to go over their notes and determine the best course of action for David. Neither of them wanted to give any credence to David's delusions of being four hundred years old and currently housing a demonic presence within his body, but they'd need to accommodate David's beliefs into their sessions. In order to get through to him, they'd need to exercise patience and caution. Once they finished up, they knew some coffee was in order.

When they arrived at the employee lounge, they found a package waiting for them. It was a sticky note attached to a DVD from Chief of Staff Harvey Wilson. It read, '*Watch me.*'

*

They went to a private viewing room, where both placed headphones over their ears. Rachel took her time examining the DVD – even though the case was completely clear – before sliding it into the player. As it began, words appeared on the screen.

Property of NSPD.

Surveillance footage obtained following discovery of the deceased.

The footage began with two men walking back and forth between the rows of seats within a church. Graphics displayed on the bottom of the screen indicated that due to a recent rash of break ins and violence towards parishioners, a state-of-the-art security system has been installed. *Not that it stopped someone from dying,* Rachel thought.

At first it appeared as though the two men were simply walking up and down the rows, but when they reached the furthest end, it became apparent that they were collecting trash. The taller man dragged a garbage can from between the rows.

"I'll take this out to the dumpster," the shorter man said.

"That's most kind of you, Father Burke, but I can manage. If you'd be so willing as to ensure the bibles are in neat order while I take this outside, that would be splendid."

As Father Burke began to move throughout the rows, adjusting and fixing the placement of the supplied bibles, the taller man proceeded to move off-camera with the garbage can.

Graphics appeared on screen to indicate he was Father Lavery.

The camera briefly changed views to show Father Lavery exiting from the back of the church. He crossed the short distance of the rear parking lot, and emptied the garbage can into the dumpster. Once done, he walked back across the parking lot, and re-entered the church. The screen changed views again, back to Father Burke who continued to work his way through the rows, adjusting the bibles as he went.

When he got to the farthest section, the lower right-hand side of the screen, he stopped abruptly. He looked around as if he'd heard something, pausing when Father Lavery re-entered the frame.

"Was that you?" Burke asked.

"Was that me... what?" Lavery replied.

"Did you just say something to me? Right before I asked if that was you?"

"No. I just got back inside. Everything ok?"

Burke shook his head, as though clearing out cobwebs.

"Must've been daydreaming," he said, resuming his duty of tidying the bibles.

"You got the time?" Lavery asked, as he stopped walking near the top of the screen.

"Yeah, it's... just after nine. You have a counseling session this morning?"

More graphics appeared on screen, informing the viewer that Father Lavery was in charge of the pre-marital counseling sessions.

"No, but I do have to get that email off to the city. The permit committee was supposed to give us an answer yesterday about whether we'd be approved for that west expansion for our music auditorium renovations. Didn't hear a thing. I just know that what's-his-name in permitting –"

"Siemens," Burke cut in.

"Yes, Siemens, that's right. If I can email him before noon, he's more likely to reply on the same day. Friendly guy, but I wish he'd do more to get this permit pushed through."

"He can only do so much."

"I know, Burke. And it's not like I can threaten him with eternal damnation, after all!"

They broke into laughter, and Lavery gave Burke a friendly wave as he left.

Burke continued to work through the rows. He was on the top left of the screen, with only three rows remaining, when a loud bang occurred. Seemingly unable to discern exactly where the sound came from, Burke jolted at the noise. The bible he was straightening flew from his hand and arced through the air before falling to the floor near the altar. The sound echoed through the pews within the nave.

"Hello?" Burke said.

Even though he was on the top of the screen and furthest from the camera, he visibly shook. He took two steps towards the center of the pews before a hoarse sound occurred. It was reminiscent of a sick person attempting to clear their throat of phlegm, and as the sound occurred, the lights in the room went out, the video screen going completely black.

"Hello?" Burke shouted. A thud sounded, followed by pained noises from Burke.

The lights suddenly came back on, illuminating Burke, who was standing between the pews, holding his right knee.

As he moved closer to the middle of the screen, it became noticeable that his knee was bleeding, his hands doing a poor job of staunching the flow.

"Lavery!"

He screamed the other Father's name, his face contorted with pain.

Burke took two more steps before flopping into the front pew..

At that point the camera switched angles, from behind the rows of pews to a side view that showcased the altar and the Presider's Chair, Credence Table, and

Tabernacle. Father Burke could still be seen, but only the first three rows of seats were on the left side of the screen.

Burke writhed in the seat, gripping his knee. Blood pooled on the floor around his feet.

"Father Burke."

At the sound of the male's voice, Burke immediately let go of his knee and sat up straight, as though nothing had happened.

"When we last met, I was but a young child. Do you know who I am?"

"No."

"Don't lie to me," the voice said, but still, no one else was visible on screen.

"When you *saved* me, you were to care for me. Do you know who I am?"

"Only a person wishing to be saved can save themselves. I play no hand in your life. I only guide."

"Don't tap dance around the answer. Do you know *who* I am?" The unseen speaker was more forceful, as though his voice was amplified through a sound system.

"I will not allow you to befoul this Holy Sanctuary," Burke replied softly, the camera barely able to pick up what he said. His voice trembled, and as he spoke, he crossed his arms over his chest.

The Unseen began to hysterically laugh at this. Still, only Burke was visible on the screen. As the laughter reached its apex, a shadow shifted near the altar. A shapeless form moved from the darkness and stopped before Burke, kneeling so that they were right in front of the man. A dark appendage slid forward, caressing Burke's wound. It was difficult to make out on the video, but the figure appeared to smear some of Burke's blood on its fingers. The appendage retreated and the sound of frantic sucking could be heard, followed by an orgasmic groan.

"God, your blood tastes divine."

The figure stood, spun around, and the formless shape danced in the shadowed footage. It abruptly stopped, and, with a flourish, the veil that concealed it was thrown back, exposing a male who looked exactly like David. Almost. He had longer hair, and something was incorrect with his legs. The knees were too far backwards, the shins pushed behind his feet at an obscene angle, as though he was part barnyard animal.

"This is NOT a Holy Sanctuary. No, far from. This is a Mourning Palace. The last place you'll ever know. Look around you. Loooooook, Burke. You see the sinners? The dead and the decayed you preach about and worship. Bah! The lot of you are horrendous blights upon the earth. I wish a swarm of locusts came upon us at this very instant to devour you and leave only your bones so that I may clean my teeth with them."

Burke rocked back in the pew, as though he was struck. His nose erupted, blood splashing across his face and down his chest. His arms reached out in an attempt to defend himself against someone, but no one was close.

"Forgive me, Father Burke, for you have sinned," David said, taking two steps towards the bloodied man. With each step there was an echoed clack, the sound of an animal's hoof striking cement. David dropped to his knees in front of Burke, the edges of his body flickering as though he was fading from view, before returning a moment later.

"When you found me, you took from me what I cherished. Where is my book?"

"Ghunnnhhhh," was all Father Burke replied, a pained sound that came from behind a layer of blood.

"When you found me, you took from me what you wanted. I want it back."

Father Burke slammed backwards against the pew again, a bloody spot appearing on the palm of each hand.

"Is this how you imagined it would end? I guess one blessing is that if I exist, maybe your God does too? I can't tell you if he does or doesn't, but I *can* tell you that your death will not be painless."

David leaned forward, grabbed Burke's left arm, and yanked it towards him. As he did this, his lower jaw seemingly unhinged itself, allowing for a predatory opening to appear. He bit down when Burke's entire hand was in his mouth, the man screaming at the top of his lungs as David pushed him back, the lower half of his arm missing. Once David swallowed, he looked directly at the camera, before biting off the lower half of Burke's right arm.

"God, that was delicious, but I'm not through yet," he said, wiping his bloody chin. "When you cared for me, do you remember how you used to try to help me fall asleep?"

Burke was blabbering. His head rolled around on his shoulders, legs spasming.

"I remember," David said, lowering his demonic head to Burke's groin and chomping down. As his teeth sliced through genitals, Burke squealed loudly, like a pig branded with a hot iron. As David continued to bite down and violently shake his head back and forth, like a dog with a chew toy playing tug with its master, Burke went limp, his head slumping backwards and turning to the side.

David continued to feast.

Onscreen text indicated that the video had been sped up to five times its usual speed.

Throughout, David was between Burke's legs, seemingly savoring the man's flesh. Fifteen minutes later, David stopped, hoisting Burke over his shoulder and disappearing off screen, moving towards the altar.

More graphics appeared, stating that thirty minutes later Father Lavery re-entered to find Father Burke's body. He was slumped against the back wall, out of the camera's view, impaled rectally on a three-foot-tall cement cross.

12.

ONCE THE SCREEN WENT black, Rachel leaned back in her chair and breathed out deeply. Darryl rubbed his eyes and looked at Rachel, making a gesture that said, *just what the fuck did we watch?*

"Clinically, I have some thoughts," said Rachel. "Should the two of us debrief before we meet with Bagg?"

"I think that's for the best. I have two patients scheduled that I need to see shortly. How about we reconvene tomorrow morning, say six? And we can approach Bagg with our suggestions before either of us see David for another session?"

"Works for me," Rachel replied, as she ejected the DVD and turned off the system. They left the room one after the other, which did a solid job of calming them both. Darryl said his goodbyes as he headed down the hallway, towards his office.

Rachel stood a minute, trying to play back what it was that they'd watched, and what it was that she had seen. She understood that these were not the same things, but she needed to do her best to compartmentalize each, and find the grey area in between to give her the closest idea of 'what happened.' Either way, she knew that David killed Father Burke in a horrific manner, but a part of her still wondered if that was *the* David on the video, the one that she'd been interviewing. She thought back to when he looked at the camera, as though he were looking at her as he prepared to do what he did. And that David – yes, *that* David, the one that seemingly knew more than he should – was there... Rachel needed to decide to what extent he was playing a part, and to what extent he was telling the truth.

And thinking about that, after having watched the footage, filled her with the deepest fear she had ever felt.

But as she prepared to go to her office, she paused, leaned back against the door to the room, needing a solid presence behind her. A flicker. There it was. Something else that she'd caught on the video. Something that she hadn't comprehended at first. As though another, larger, figure had also been present when David had appeared onscreen. She shuddered, goosebumps covering her arms. There *had* been another presence there.

Not only that, but she also remembered what David had asked of Father Burke. It would be something she'd need to ask him about in their next meeting.

When you found me, you took from me what I cherished. Where is my book?

She immediately thought back to an interview she'd conducted with Father Gio only a few weeks after David had arrived.

*

Rachel sat across from Father Gio in an intake room.

"Have you had the chance to review David Stewart's file, Father?"

"I have," he replied.

"From your perspective, what did you think from reading the notes? What are your initial thoughts?"

Father Gio pursed his lips before offering a false smile. Rachel had seen this before when someone was taking their time to reply. It drove her crazy, but she remained calm and patient, as she always did.

"I understand this is within a professional setting, otherwise I wouldn't have access to such confidential material. I appreciate you bringing me on. With your permission, I'd like to also have the secondary opinion of Father Matthew Anderson. We can make the arrangements once done here."

"Yes, that will be fine. But, Father, what were your initial thoughts?" she asked, wondering why the man was stalling.

Father Gio smiled, eyes dropping away from Rachel's before returning to match her gaze.

"As a man of faith... I struggled. We've suspected 'demonic' possession to be nothing more than hyperactivity of certain medical conditions for many years. I know the Church in general has a horrible reputation among non-believers. I understand the desire to use a few 'bad apples' to describe the majority of the flock, which pains me to no end. Truth be told, 'demonic possession' or similar sensationalized events are nothing more than that. Undiagnosed schizophrenia. Manic mood swings. Bipolar disruptions. We trust in the medical community to diagnose and treat so that we can continue living our lives and devoting our time to the Lord and Savior," he said, a look of smugness crossing his face.

"Yes, that is a noted historical element. But again, you are doing your best to dance around what I've asked." If she could smack him, she would. Really show him that he's not above her, and that all she wanted was for him to answer the fucking question. It was only then, when she looked at him, that she noticed something. His bottom lip quivered almost imperceptibly.

"Maybe, I'm stalling because what I've read and seen has shaken me more than I should allow."

"In what way?" Rachel asked.

"Are you familiar with the Bible?"

"No, I'll admit that I am not," she said.

"Have you ever read it?"

"No."

Father Gio waved his hand at her. The motion could be taken as either 'don't worry about it,' or as a way of Gio indicating he was annoyed. She didn't care either way, she just wanted him to explain what he meant.

"Then I will simplify. So, the general public is told that the Devil is a personification of evil. That there was this rising up of 'evil' to try and achieve the same level of power as God. So, in response, God cast out the Devil, or this fallen angel, who was sent down. Depending on how far you go with this story, he either ends up on earth and tries to fight his way back to Heaven, or the Devil ends up in Hell where he anoints himself Lord and rules the souls of the sinners."

"Yes, I'm following," she said.

"Well, what if I told you – and this is where Father Anderson would come in, he being more of an expert than I – that there are others who believe something very different? Others who understand the world on a... Celestial level."

"This I *don't* follow," Rachel said, shifting in her chair to sit straighter.

"In 1904, Aleister Crowley was in Egypt furthering his beliefs when he described a voice that began to speak to him. He said this was a messenger of Horus, the God of the Sky. He copied down everything that this voice said to him over the next three days, April eight, ninth, and tenth. This became Liber AL vel Legis or The Book of the Law. The central sacred text of Thelema. This noted work opened the eyes of many to the potential of Cosmic Gods. Those beyond our own Lord, who come from above and preside over us through cosmic immortality."

"What does that mean?" Rachel said, trying to follow along but not fully connecting the dots.

"That those Gods are always there, always made of cosmic matter, and that when the eleven of them return, those who believe will ascend. This wasn't exactly the Thelema that Crowley developed, but from there, other groups of people have branched away from it and began to worship their own deities. I only mention this because were one to research Crowley and Thelema, they will find differences. I want to make that clear for the records."

"Noted. And what does this have to do with our patient?" she asked.

"You have spent significant time with Mr. Stewart, have you not?"

"I've met with him daily since his arrival. Some days the session has been less than ten minutes, others closer to six hours. It all depends on if Mr. Stewart is cooperative that day or not."

"And in this time, have you noticed anything unusual about him?" Father Gio asked.

"Professionally and personally, I am unable to answer that. We deal with all kinds of significant diagnoses here from patients who come from all walks of life. I am here to get to know each and every patient and find the best path to helping them be as healthy – and safe – as possible."

"That's not what I meant. I apologize. Have you looked into his eyes? Really looked at them. Has anything odd occurred with his hands? His walking. Anything *unusual* with his gait?"

"Nothing I've noted. I'm also there as an impartial professional. I don't judge a patient for how they walk, look, or move," Rachel said.

"That's not what I mean. Look, has this patient scared you? Not frightened you, or done something to make you jump or move back rapidly, but honest to goodness scared you deep within here?" Father Gio jabbed a finger roughly into his chest. He shifted in his seat, adjusting his glasses before they toppled off his nose.

"No, at this stage I can honestly say I haven't experienced anything like that."

Father Gio nodded his head. Rachel thought that his expression suggested he didn't believe her.

"Have you been in a room with him, just the two of you, but you could've sworn someone else was there?" the priest asked.

Rachel looked at the older man for almost a minute without speaking. Before she said anything, he leaned forward, closer towards her.

"Dr. Hoggendorf, what you need to understand here, is that there is something significantly wrong with the patient you know as David Stewart. He is not of this place. He is but a vessel for something behind the veil. Be careful. If it gets out... just be careful."

13.

RACHEL SMILED WARMLY AT David as he was led into the interview room. David watched her expressionlessly, even after the guard had seated him and moved away. Then, as though a light switch had been flipped, his face broke out into an enormous, comical smile, teeth exposed.

"How're you today, David?"

"Great! This place is pretty swell," he said excitedly.

"You seem to be in good spirits? Getting better sleep?"

David laughed, the unexpectedness of it causing Rachel to jump in her seat.

"Did I make a joke?"

"Spirits. Oh, Rachel, you are just so mischievous," he said.

"I'm sorry, I'm not following," she replied, analyzing his face.

David waved his hand.

"Ok, so you've been here just over a month. How do you feel you are settling in?"

"I live in a cell. A room. Padded walls. I spend all my time there unless I'm here with you. Or that one hour I get to walk around outside in the fenced yard. It's not as though I'm attending college."

"Yes, but from where you came from, this must be a significant change, surely? While you may lack freedom, I'd suspect – at least based on what you've said – that you feel safer here."

"Safer? I'm not safe anywhere," he replied with a low chuckle.

"How so?"

"I exist here *and* there. And while I'm away from what I need, I can't see up *there*, I still feel it. Don't you?"

"Don't I what?"

"What if I told you I was there."

"Where?" Rachel said, feeling as though the air in the room had thickened and grown hot.

"When *it* happened. Your attack. *Momma*," the last word spoken as though a child was across from Rachel.

"David, this is off track," Rachel said, knowing she looked visibly shaken. She shifted in her seat several times, crossing her legs, before she placed her notepad on her lap again and looked at David.

"I know what happened at that party. When you were in high school."

"David, how 'bout we discuss what programs you'd like to join while you're here? You haven't selected any options. You've not even filled out the list to let the librarian know what genre of books you'd like to borrow."

"I have no need for *those* books." David replied, raising his voice slightly.

"What do you have a need for?"

For a moment, Rachel thought she had unsettled him. She'd experienced it dozens of times in her career, that split second internally where the patient across from her has to decide if they lash out or remain seated. It didn't bother her one way or the other. Progress was only made when she had the patient communicating, which was what David was doing. She watched his face closely, and saw a thin smile replace the frown he had worn only moments before.

"How did it make you feel that he died? Different than when he slipped in so easily. At first you were so surprised. *How could that be?* You didn't want it, but there it was, deep inside where no one else had ever been. You cried after he left. But then that poor lad... such a shame. He had a bright future ahead of him. That's what the principal said at the school when they had the memorial for him, didn't he?"

"How..." Rachel began, but David cut her off, continuing.

"And you were forced to go to that assembly. Sit there while your friends cried. They were so sad that he'd died. Meanwhile, you were still bleeding and sore. And then came the positive test. But you couldn't tell anyone. You'd have been tarred and feathered – saying a dead kid had raped you at a party and knocked you up. How did that make *you* feel? Hmmm? How, Rachel? Like a slut? Like a failure? He was a shining beacon at your school. Wasn't he?"

Rachel stood, looking at David, before leaving the room. Once she'd gone, David remained. He continued smiling, which transformed as he broke into a giggling fit, before it became hysterical laughter. And he was still laughing when the two orderlies came to return him to his room.

14.

Did I ever tell you about my mother, Dr. Dravendash?

I didn't?

Well, that's silly. How could I not have told you about my mother!

I grew up in a great neighborhood; great parents, great everything. Textbook, some would say. I was popular; I played every sport and won all kinds of awards.

I was that kid that people hated in school because I could get away with whatever I wanted.

My father was super protective of me. He knew what others wanted from me; you could see the lust in the other dads' eyes when I was around. It wasn't anything I paid attention to, no not me, but it was there, this lingering *haze* of testosterone.

If I were to wear a bikini in front of them, they'd have to sit, hiding the bulges that tented their shorts. I saw it a few times, always laughed. I wasn't interested in that at all, not back when it was happening.

When I was sixteen, my classmate, the quarterback of the football team, raped me at a party. After the rape, he left, drunk, and crashed his car. He died in that crash.

As a result of that rape, I became pregnant. Oh, how it ripped my parents' hearts out. Their little girl, pregnant! They forbade me from carrying it at all. My dad drove me to the clinic where I had an abortion.

Did it hurt?

I think it did, Darryl, but I can't remember. Oh, I'm not to call you Darryl? Whatever you say Dr. Dravendash. I remember when we were on a first name basis. And now, because I'm in here, we can't be?

Oh, no, I get it. Doctor-Patient boundaries, I'm aware.

So, after graduating high school, I went to university. I graduated with honors and had scholarships galore. I lived on-campus and made so many friends, but it was one friend, Richard, who intrigued me the most. He was so different from the rest of my straight-laced friends. He wore black clothes everywhere, black nail polish, eye liner and lipstick. He was a genius, and would only come to a few classes a week. Even then, he was acing every exam we took.

What does this have to do with my mom? I'm getting there.

Now, in the third year of my five-year program – I was expediting two degrees before challenging my master's program – we planned a trip for our reading break that spring. There were going to be a dozen of us when we planned it, but when it came time to go, there were four who went – myself, Richard and my two friends, Heidi and Kelly. Both liked Richard, but neither were overly fond of him coming. I assured them it would be fine.

Anyways, our initial plan had been to go to Switzerland, but when only four of us confirmed, we switched and decided to go to Poland. Richard's parents were from Poland, and after some back and forth, we were able to arrange to stay with his family and friends over in Poland. That meant that we'd have free accommodations for the trip, which was huge for us!

The first few days were magical. We walked through the streets of Warsaw, ate so much amazing food, and laughed until the sun came up.

But an odd thing occurred.

Richard insisted we see a particular place. He practically demanded it.

It was Zofiówka Sanatorium in Otwock. We travelled by bus before walking to this decrepit, broken-down place. Heidi and Kelly were mortified when they first saw it, Kelly going so far as to threaten to turn around and go straight to the airport. But Richard insisted that we go in as he needed to show us something we just had to see.

The place wasn't guarded or gated, so we just walked right in. The two girls were antsy, but I was on cloud nine. The second I saw the place, the graffiti on the walls disappeared, and the cobble stone that had collapsed seemingly rebuilt itself. It had been raining all day, but once there, it was as though the sky had cleared and the sun shone down just for me. Richard noticed it, kept looking at me, smiling. It was the first time I'd ever noticed Richard giving me a lustful look. Not a sexual thing, but as though he saw me in a different light and was completely enamored with me. He knew. He understood that I could see what he could see.

The shroud he wore was also lifted.

It was as though by entering this place, Richard had become a completely different person, just as much as the building itself had changed.

I reached out to hold his hand, my breath hitching when he clutched it back. His face had become sunken, his eyes sitting deeper in his skull. The hooves that adorned the ends of his legs echoed throughout the hallway as we walked, the clicking and the clacking creating a rhythm that seemed to arouse me to the point of orgasm, but not letting me tip over the edge.

He pulled me along, the two others completely forgotten. I didn't see them again until we were back at school. We were going to fly home on the same flight, but they must've changed theirs. I said hello in that first class back, but both only looked at me before changing seats, and we never spoke again.

Anyways, back in the sanatorium, Richard led me, and I followed. At first, we walked, before we sped up, our feet almost floating over the debris on the floor as we raced down the green overgrown hallways. After a series of turns, we came to a darkened door. All around the frame of open blackness that lived between were graffitied hands, some human, some clawed. As my eyes took in the level of detail, I swore I could see them flex and shift, as though alive. At the same time, Richard squeezed my hand tighter, and I could feel his fingernails break through the skin of my palms, the pain but a quick inhalation accompanied by a sharp noise. It was his way of telling me he was the same as those hands that surrounded that entrance. Something shimmered within the darkness. I could make out the details of the hallway behind, but I could also see *things* moving, beasts not of this world walking around before they stopped and looked at us, seeing us from their side of the void.

"In there," I said. It wasn't so much as a question for Richard, but a statement. He'd led me here and we were going to go in there.

"Please," Richard said.

His reply was emotionless, devoid of his usual tone, that cadence I'd grown to recognize as the way he spoke. This was more robotic than anything, as though speaking through the mud of a dream.

I took a step forward, Richard remaining where he was, our hands still clasped together. As I got to the point where the shimmering fluid that filled the open area of the door was less than an inch from my face, he let go of my hand, and, before I could react, I heard him rush forward, his hooves banging against the floor, and he slammed into me, both of us flying forward into the chaos of discovery.

Part Three

Chaos

15.

THE STARS.

That's what I remember most.

Do you remember the first time you saw a shooting star? Or when the constellations came into focus, and you could actually see a soldier or any of the animals?

I saw it all and more within the few seconds that we went into the void and arrived on the other side.

We hit the ground hard, no longer in the abandoned building. I struggled to get up at first, the impact having knocked the air from my lungs. I was helped up by the hands that had been around the door. I couldn't believe what I was seeing when I was finally on my feet. A single humanoid with dozens of arms stood, towering over me. Its face had no features, just a smooth place where its eyes and mouth and nose should've been. It moaned when I looked, which I took to as a greeting. I smiled back, allowing its many hands to roam my body. When they descended below my waist and felt my legs, it shuddered and stepped backwards. Richard moaned from the ground, sounding like he was in pain, but when he did it again, I understood he was communicating. The humanoid's hands explored Richard, and when it felt his odd legs and hooves, it moaned again and beckoned for us to follow.

"You're almost home," Richard said, as we started after the creature. "Just a little further."

We walked behind this gargantuan figure, birds chirping in the trees and the sun dancing through the forest canopy to shine upon us as we went. The air was pristine, the surroundings picture-perfect.

I'd never felt as though I'd ever belonged anywhere else more than right there in my life. I was happy, I was full of love, and I watched as the creature and Richard stepped into a clearing and the reality of what lay beyond what we can see came into view and everything changed.

*

May I have some water?

Thank you. Dr. Dravendash, are you sweating?

Just looks like you're sweating. Is it because of me? Or what I'm telling you?

No, I took that trip. It happened. What do you mean there's no record of me attending the school? Well, how did I get my degrees? No, I don't remember going there. *No*, that was not the school I attended. Maybe they made a mistake when they printed my degree?

Does David ever appear in your dreams?

You want me to go on?

Ok, if you insist.

*

Ash.

The clearing was covered in a thin layer of ash.

From above, a light downfall of the filament fell, creating a dense coating within my mouth. As I licked the inside with my tongue, I began to taste copper and when the fluid filled that space, I let the dark liquid escape from between my lips and cascade down my chin. It wasn't until it had all poured forth that I understood most of my teeth had come loose and threatened to pop free if I worked them any harder with my tongue.

Within the middle of the clearing, I could see a writhing mass of dirt and mud-covered people in an orgiastic ball of carnal acts. It resembled a den of snakes as they mated, things being thrust in and pulled out no matter where my eyes fell. The sounds they made were as grating as the smell that permeated from the ball of sweat and fluids.

Surrounding the rutting mass of soiled participants stood eleven beasts.

These figures were from the deepest, darkest recesses of my mind, and as I looked at each one and took in the aura that emanated from them, I knew I was looking at the oldest and most powerful *things* to ever have stepped foot on this planet.

"The eleven cosmic chaos Gods," Richard said to me. "They are your parents, our parents, and now you are home."

Before I knew what I was doing, I'd removed my clothes and waded into the sea of filth. Immediately something stiff entered my mouth. I wrapped my lips around the thick, veiny member and began to suck and slurp to my heart's content. A finger entered me and began to slide in and out. Soon, another finger entered, and another. It should've hurt, but instead I felt full, and bobbed my head faster and harder on the delicious dick in my mouth. As this continued, I felt something penetrate my ass. This put me over the edge, and I came hard. At the same time, my nipples began to leak, but I paid no attention. I was so focused on finishing whoever this was in my mouth. After they came, I swallowed, wiped my lips, and found another, beginning to suck on a new cock. More fingers invaded me, more lips sucked on me, and tongues licked me. It was a never-ending carnival of fluid and fucking.

For how long this went on, I don't know. It finally ended when a chime sounded, and we all immediately stopped. I felt something wither and flop from between my legs. What had been thrusting into my ass bulged and released before it was pulled free. I let go of what I was stroking in my right hand and let what was in my mouth leave, my tongue continuing to lick it until it was too far away. Everything drained from everywhere. The chime came again, and we all stood, as though under some sort of unseen power.

I should've felt vulnerable standing there naked and leaking, or perhaps ashamed... but I felt invigorated, and longing to return to the throng of ecstasy.

"My children," one of them said, moving forwards on thick, sucker-covered tentacles. "The time for obedience and worship is upon you." It slid closer to the bearded male beside me and wrapped a tentacle around his stomach, pulling him close before disappearing with him into the ash.

*

What do you mean?

But I don't understand what you mean?

No, I didn't take any drugs or hallucinogens.

Dr. Dravendash, you've known me for how long?

No, shut up. Shut your fucking mouth, you asshole. YOU KNOW ME. IT'S ME! FUCK. I'm not making anything up, this all happened and trust me when I say this, it's going to happen to you. David has his eye on you. The one that David carries with him knows you want to experience this. We all know...

Let me go on, please? Yes, I'm begging you. Why won't you talk to me!! No... no you're not talking to me; you're talking *at* me. Big difference.

Look, I want to prepare you, ok?

*

I knew which one of the beasts that surveyed us would be mine.

How could I not?

I watched, as, one by one, the horned and hoofed figures stepped forward and selected one of the participants from the debauchery. Some were not chosen. Some were beheaded or devoured before the person standing on either side was whisked away screaming into the void.

When it was my turn, I was struggling to remain still, knowing that even the slightest movement might result in my death. I was confident Richard hadn't brought me here to be killed, but if this was a test, I needed to make sure I passed.

An immense beast circled around those remaining, sizing each of them up. I knew she was for me. I felt it in my heart and by how wet my pussy became. The fluid began to leak from my sore and abandoned hole, dribbling down my inner thighs so that by the time she stood directly in front of me, it had coated me all the way to the knees.

"You smell delicious," she said, licking her lips.

In normal circumstances, I would've been repulsed. Here I was, longing for this twenty-foot-tall *thing*, this nightmare with thick, fur-covered legs, giant leathery wings that folded and unfolded behind her, blotting out the darkness each time they did. Her face had changed when she stopped to talk to me. When I'd first seen it, it had been scaled, fanged, and covered in pustules that burst when she shifted her expression. Now, she had the face of a goddess, delicate features with lips that shone and begged for me to kiss. I gasped as she reached out and inserted a thick finger into my pussy, my insides grabbing hold and squeezing against the intrusion.

"Yes, you'll do just fine," she said.

I leaned forward, taking her grotesquely large right nipple into my mouth, and began to feed ravenously, as though I was just born and fresh from the womb needing nourishment.

*

What happened next?

I'm not sure.

I had witnessed the others get taken, but for me it never happened.

The next thing I remembered was waking up with Richard sitting beside me in the woods, behind the abandoned building. My clothes were back on but I felt dirty and... violated.

We walked back to our hotel, neither of us speaking. A few times I looked over at Richard, who only raised his eyebrows when he saw me looking, as though to say 'see, I told you it would be magical,' but he never said a word.

At the hotel, I showered and climbed into bed, finding it odd that the girls were gone. Then I went to sleep.

When I woke up, I was on the floor, here in the interview room, with David looming over me as the alarms blared and people were pounding on the door to get in.

16.

Doctor Darryl Dravendash, Father Matthew Anderson, and Carl Bagg MD, Head of the Institution all sat in Bagg's office. There was a camera in the corner of the room, affixed to the ceiling. They knew this meeting must be recorded, considering the escalation of recent events, but none of them were happy to be there. All three appeared agitated, Father Anderson bouncing his left leg over his right leg while frequently checking his watch. Dr. Dravendash had a notepad on his lap, but his pen was clenched between his teeth.

"This meeting will be on the record. Saying that, I need to know what in the *fuck* happened to Doctor Rachel Hoggendorf," Carl said, immediately shifting in his office chair that groaned in protest at the sudden movement.

Dravendash let out a long breath, plucked the pen from between his teeth, and proceeded to tap it against the notepad as though it were a miniature drumstick. His face looked pained, as if each breath were linked to a shock collar around his neck.

"I don't know. Truly, I've never seen anything like this. Can't find any literature that comes close," Dravendash replied with a stuntedness that relayed how uncomfortable he was.

"I can offer an opinion... but... I'm not sure you'll be accepting of my hypothesis," Anderson said.

"Hypothesis? Science-based shit from a man of the cloth?" Bagg said, which normally might've elicited a laugh from the men.

"You'd be surprised."

"Would I?" Bagg replied, his shoulders bunching.

"Easy fellas. This doesn't need to be about who has a bigger dick or whatever you two are growing hostile about. We need to help Rachel," Dravendash said, trying to ease the tension that had already begun to spill over in the room.

"I'm afraid that, much like David, Rachel is beyond help," Anderson said.

"What does that mean?" Bagg replied.

"I've read the transcription of her interview with you, Darryl. Her description of what occurred on her 'trip,' whether she ever actually went on said trip, is startlingly accurate to what some members of a strange cult we've become aware of have described in their works."

"What cult?" Bagg said, and leaned in closer, as though he wanted to be filled in on a secret.

"There's a known group of people who actively attempt to achieve immortality. They believe that by calling back to earth the eleven cosmic chaos gods, they'll ascend to a land of ash where they can participate in carnal depravity for the rest of time," Anderson said with dead seriousness.

"That does sound horrifically similar to what Rachel described," Dravendash said.

"It does," Anderson said with a nod. "After reading the transcript, I reached out to a colleague who sent me various accounts of their activities over the decades. They oddly fell off the grid over the last few years, which could very well correlate to David's claims that he has been possessed by one of them. If he has *actually* been, that would explain why the members are silent – they've gone underground in preparation to ascend."

"Jesus Christ, do you hear yourself? Are you honestly suggesting that our patient is possessed and that Dr. Hoggendorf is telling the truth?" Bagg said, breathing out.

"Look, I know it's difficult for you to believe. Trust me, I can appreciate how this sounds from your side of the table, but you need to understand, this is something I've studied for many years," Anderson said. Dravendash appreciated how neutral the man was remaining, how even-keeled, considering he could see just how worked up his suggestions were making Carl.

"I don't know if I can accept that. Saying that, I want to do what is best for both of our patients. Fuck, does that sting to consider Rachel as one our patients," Dravendash said, shaking his head.

"Get used to it," Bagg said. "This morning she managed to cut off all her hair and ingested it. She was screaming that her mother told her she needed to do it."

"Did she carve any markings on her body, or anything on the walls?" Anderson asked.

"Not that I'm aware of, but I'll get confirmation for you," Bagg said.

"Anderson... I don't know how to ask this without sounding completely insane. But is there anything I can do to protect myself from whatever is afflicting David and Rachel?" Dravendash asked.

When Bagg didn't reply, Anderson spoke.

"Well, I see two sides to that," Anderson said. "On the one hand, you've all been perpetuating that this is simply a case of mental illness, that David was suffering from schizophrenia or bipolar disorder. Even multiple personality disorders have been mentioned. So, if that is the case, that's not something you can *catch*, correct? Those are not things given to others like the common cold. And if it is just mental illness, as you've been trying to state, that doesn't explain what has happened to Rachel. Unless she's succumbed to overwhelming stress and her coping mechanism is to mimic or recreate what David is going through."

"Ok, and what's on the other end of this arrogant observation?" Bagg asked.

"Well, the other side would be the argument that states you currently have two patients within the confirms of your facility that are categorically possessed. And, if you accept that they are, that will change your approach to patient care, but would also allow for certain *things* to be put into place to theoretically protect yourself."

"Oh, come off it already. Are you honestly taking us down this road?" Bagg replied, his hand absently reaching out and gripping the handle of his coffee cup so hard his knuckles went white. Dravendash was surprised the handle didn't break, especially considering he knew full well Bagg was pretending the handle was Anderson's neck.

"Nothing's making sense here, Carl. I would rather be prudent and make sure I don't end up babbling about space monster cocks in my ass."

"Normally, I'd rip you a new one for what you just said, but I'll allow it. But keep your tongue in check here, Darryl. We're still professionals and we're still trying to treat these patients with the utmost ability while in our care," Bagg said. Darryl was happy to see that Carl's mouth had broken into a half-smirk, the attempt at levity getting through just a bit.

"I apologize."

"When do you next meet with David or Rachel?" Anderson asked.

"I have a session with David this afternoon. That is, if I'm still going to be seeing him?" Dravendash said, looking at Carl.

"Absolutely," Carl replied.

"Would I be able to observe?" Anderson asked.

"Any hesitation, Carl?" Dravendash said.

"You gonna have those protections in place?" he said with a heavy dose of sarcasm. "I don't want you both having to be hauled out by guards."

"They will."

"Then I see no issue. As long as you have no problem with it, Darryl?" Bagg asked.

"None on my end. Let's meet at one-thirty, the session starts at two," Dravendash replied.

"Sounds good," Anderson replied. He got up and shook Bagg's hand and nodded at Darryl, before leaving the room.

"Shut that camera off on your way out, Darryl," Bagg said as Darryl stood. "I need a drink."

17.

ANDERSON WAS WAITING PROMPTLY for Darryl at one-thirty outside the interview room. As usual, Darryl thought the man looked nervous. They chatted briefly, both having mentally prepared for whatever it was that David would be throwing at them. When they heard the clinking of cuffs coming towards them from around the corner, they went into the room and sat.

When David was led in, cuffed around his wrists and legs, he appeared surprised to see the two men, but his eyes twinkled with an excitement that suggested he was all for whatever today's session would bring.

"These stay on," the orderly remarked, referring to the wrist and ankle restraints. He helped David get seated and comfortable before he went and leaned against the back wall.

"Understood," Dravendash replied.

"Father Anderson," David said. "Nice to see you today. Are you here to learn the truth?"

"Good afternoon, David," Dravendash said.

"Was I fucking talking to you, scum?" David stared at Darryl before returning to look at Anderson.

"I'm just here to observe," Anderson replied, smiling warmly.

"*As I was saying*, did you want to learn the truth?"

"About what?" Darryl asked.

David looked at Darryl, glaring. "About all of this. Where we sit. Where you walk when you leave the facility. What is above your head when the sun disappears."

Darryl smirked. "Sure. Enlighten us."

"Sarcasm? Really?" David said, still focusing his attention on Father Anderson.

"I apologize, David, that wasn't my intention."

"Apology accepted," David said before going silent. He dropped his head, his eyes focused on the cuffs around his wrists.

"Are you not going to speak anymore this session, David?" Dravendash asked.

"I am preparing you for the truth."

Father Anderson nodded at Darryl before saying, "And that is?"

"That nothing awaits those who don't believe. That I was bound to walk this path. At first forced by possession but ultimately giving over to what awaits me. But what awaits you two? Nothing? Maybe you'll come around, Dr. Dravendash, but Father Anderson will be fucked and eaten and then left to decompose on the ground he dies upon."

"Many people believe that once we die, that's it," Dravendash said. "Nothing. Over. Others believe that there is a Heaven and a Hell. If someone believes in demons, they must, by default, believe in God and Heaven and Hell. They go part and parcel, wouldn't you say?"

"I'm not talking about what people read about in that phoney book they only obey on Sundays. I'm talking about this path that I am bound to walk. That what awaits me, what awaits those who believe and those who have been... infused with the energy needed, will leave here, and go *there*." David said. He looked up, pointing both hands to the ceiling above. Father Anderson followed where he was pointing, but Dr. Dravendash didn't take his eyes off David.

"What happened to Dr. Hoggendorf?" Dravendash asked.

"Rachel." David let out a long sigh, shaking his head back and forth. "Dear Rachel. She wanted me to penetrate her. You know that? From the first time we met, I knew she lusted to have *this* inside her. And now that it's in her... she's changed, hasn't she? For the better."

"How did you do it?" Father Anderson asked.

"Do what?" David replied.

"I don't believe Dr. Hoggendorf is faking or pretending to have become afflicted by something for attention," Dravendash said. "She's one of the most highly regarded practitioners in her field. After thinking long and hard about it, I believe she is suffering the same as you, David. What I'm saying is that I believe you two are possessed by *something*. What? I'm not able to determine that. But I do believe multiple personalities are fighting within you both, and I want to do my best to help you focus and get the help you need."

David laughed loudly, slapping his hands on his thighs, the chains of the cuffs clanking.

"There's no determining anything. This isn't a diagnosis-incident. This is real. This is true. And this is happening right. Before. Your. Fucking. Eyes. Open them, *Darryl*. Allow them to see what you are so steadfastly refusing to allow them to see." David grew animated. The lights flickered twice. Dr. Dravendash and Father Anderson both looked at the ceiling. David remained still. When the lights flickered a third time, he turned and stared at Father Anderson. The lights flickered one more time, and then the room went dark.

"Stay where you are, David." Darryl said, feeling small and afraid, as though an assailant was about to attack. "Father Anderson, remain calm. The back-up lights will come on momentarily."

But instead of the lights coming on, a loud animal roared, close enough that Darryl felt spit hit his forehead. Father Anderson yelled, and Darryl heard the pain in his voice, but was unable to locate where the man should be sitting. They'd only been a foot apart, at most, but Darryl found nothing when he waved his hand towards where Anderson had been. The sound of furniture legs skidding across the floor occurred, followed by the racket of chairs being thrown about and groans of pain. Several animals joined in, as though a mix of chimpanzee, hyena, and elephant noises had been made into a quick sound bite. There was another pained shout, as the lights flickered and came back on.

"Where is he?" Darryl asked, looking around the room. "Where is he?" A noise grabbed Darryl's attention. He found Father Anderson slumped against the overturned couch where David had been sitting. His head bobbed around, eyes not focusing on anything, and his chin was caked with blood, which covered his neck and the front of his suit jacket.

There was no sign of David.

"Father Anderson? Father? Can you hear me?" Darryl asked, as he walked over and knelt beside the man. As though in reply, Anderson made noises, but no words came. Darryl watched as the man shifted, a red pool behind his head coming into view. The sight of the blood set something off inside Darryl. He turned and looked at the security guard who remained frozen against the back wall, eyes wide open.

"Hey! Hey! I need help! Call for help!"

The man didn't move, his body remaining stiff as a board. Darryl watched as a thick line of drool left the side of his mouth and flowed down his chin. Realizing that the guard couldn't help him in his current state, he ran to the door and hit the panic button. Immediately an alarm began to blare, and two red lights swirled and flashed in the room.

"Eeee ippppd ohhhff mmmuuhhh huuuuunnnggg."

Darryl looked back over at Father Anderson. That man had tried to say something, but he was unable to understand it at all. Hoping he'd try to say something again, Darryl watched the man. Instead of speaking, Father Anderson began to convulse. Spitting up blood, his body wracked and bounced against the floor. Darryl had no idea what he was supposed to do. His mind was going to a million places at once. Suddenly, the door burst open and two guards entered, which worked to calm Darryl.

"Over there. Father Anderson's hurt and I can't find the patient. Lock down the facility."

The first guard examined the room as though to confirm what Darryl had said, before he held up his walkie-talkie and spoke. "Code Red, I repeat, Code Red. Facility lock down."

The red lights in the room turned off, but the alarm continued to blare. The guard walked around the room, examining the space while the second guard attended to Father Anderson.

"Oh fuck. What the hell? His tongue's gone. It looks like it was bitten off," he said as he propped open Father Anderson's mouth. Doing so caused more blood to pour out over the man's chin.

An orderly arrived at the door, going straight to the guard and Father Anderson. The orderly talked briskly with the guard, but Darryl heard nothing, the alarm making their words indiscernible. He watched as the orderly left the room for a moment, before returning with a stretcher.

With the help of the guard, the orderly lifted Father Anderson onto the stretcher and began to push him towards the door. As he did so, the alarm chirped oddly, and the lights went out once more. They remained off for less than a second, but when the lights turned back on, Father Anderson was no longer on the stretcher.

Part Four

Конец

18.

IN THE AFTERMATH OF the disappearances of Father Anderson and patient David Stewart, Carl Bagg called an emergency meeting.

Within two hours, he was seated at a table with Doctor Victor Hamesl, Specialist in Psychiatry, Harvey Wilson, Chief of Staff, and Dr. Darryl Dravendash. Father Mattia Gio called in via Skype and was able to see the proceedings using Bagg's phone propped up against a metal water bottle.

*

Over the last hour, Dr. Rachel Hoggendorf had been moved from her cell to the medical area. Much to Dr. Hamesl's dismay, he was forced to subdue her with high-powered tranquilizers and restraints. A quick video analysis showed that less than one second after the lights came back on, revealing that Father Anderson was no longer on the stretcher, Rachel had started screaming at the top of her lungs and running full-tilt into the walls, smashing her head over and over.

The first orderly that had rushed into her cell to try and stop her was immediately attacked. Rachel shrieked and leapt onto him, tearing him limb from limb. The second orderly had remained rooted to the spot, unable to go in and try to help his co-worker, and unable to flee to get additional help. He was forced from his stupor when, with the entrails of the first orderly hanging from her mouth, Rachel had pounced on him. She dragged him into the cell, while he was begging for mercy, and made short work of him.

It had been another fifteen minutes before a guard had happened by, unaware that orderlies had been dispatched to Rachel's cell. When he came upon the open door, a smell hit him. Looking in, he found Rachel sitting in the corner, her wrists bound by what turned out to be the flayed scrotal skin from both men.

"I can't be trusted. Not anymore," she'd said to the guard, who had called for backup and approached her tentatively. She didn't struggle as the guard clicked the metal handcuffs in place and helped her to her feet. Once standing, chunks of skin and muscle had sloughed from her white institution shirt. The guard had done his best to not gag, to not show weakness in front of her, but he was unable to hold it back when he finally noticed the excavated body cavities of the two orderlies.

Bagg had arrived as Rachel was being led out. When he saw the carnage within, he covered his mouth and looked at her with sorrow-filled eyes.

"What did you do, Rachel?" he asked in disbelief.

"Carl... I couldn't help it... it took over and I couldn't stop it."

Bagg had trouble even believing that the person speaking to him was Dr. Rachel Hoggendorf. She'd always been so meticulous with her makeup and hair. She was a stunner, one of the most attractive – and successful – psychologists he'd ever met. But the person he was talking to was so far removed from that career woman that it hurt him to see. She was almost completely bald; only a sparse patch of brown hair over her left ear remained. The right side of her face was swollen and red from where she'd bashed her head repeatedly against the cell wall, and her eye was closed over, purple and looking like the slightest touch would cause it to burst. Blood was caked and hardened under her nose and around her upper lip. How her nose wasn't broken was beyond him. The lower half of her face was also covered in dried blood and strands of viscera, the remnants of the two orderlies she'd consumed.

When he took more of her in, it filled him with sadness to see how far off the deep end she'd gone in such a short time. She was tear-streaked, not even a stitch of makeup. Her white shirt was covered in blood and multi-colored smears; what *that* was he didn't want to know. He'd worked at the institution in one way or another for thirty years, and seen a lot in his time, but this recent string of events was far beyond anything he'd ever experienced. He noticed two red splotches on the front of her shirt that appeared to be getting larger and spreading across the material.

"What's happened here?" he asked a nurse.

"Sir, she bit her nipples off. We haven't found them so we're assuming she's ingested them, just like she did with her hair."

Carl heard the nurse and let his eyes travel from the two red patches back to Rachel's eyes. When they connected, he didn't see the almost forty-year-old doctor. No, instead he was looking into the eyes of a frightened child, one who'd experienced something far beyond their years and didn't know how to process it.

"Help me, Carl," she said in a low voice, one that sounded as though it was on the precipice of cracking.

Before he could reply, she blinked, and in place of the scared child's eyes, he was looking into the burning embers of hatred. Of eyes not belonging to Rachel.

"Come closer, businessman. Whip out that skinny cock and let me bite it off. I'll savor it as I chew."

Carl stepped back and pushed her towards the nurse.

"Get her into solitary. Restrain her as necessary."

He watched as she was led away, Rachel's eye's remaining on his, her tongue licking her lips repulsively.

*

"I'm struggling to really process what's happened over the course of time that David Stewart has been a patient of ours," Carl said, leaning back in his chair and rubbing his eyes.

"If I may," Father Gio said, from the image displayed on the propped-up phone. "Father Anderson was an expert on this... particular subsect of 'dark religion.' It was something that the church would do, have members who specialized in looking into these practices and seeking out those who practice it, so that we could stay one step ahead of this evil. Father Anderson knew the risks when he became involved, but I don't think even he thought it would go this far," he said, shaking his head.

"This far?" Dr. Hamesl said.

"Transportation," Father Gio replied.

"Excuse me? Transportation? Surely, you're not meaning what I think you mean," Wilson said, leaning forward in his chair.

"I am."

"Look, Wilson, I was in that room," Dr. Dravendash said. "I've been around this patient and discussed in great detail with Rachel about his mannerisms and machinations. Something has never been right about David. Something was off. I put it aside to maintain my professional viewpoint, but after all that has occurred, I think he was speaking his truth, and a truth that has proven to be reality." He looked rattled, as though he'd been hit by a bag of flour and not all of it had washed off.

"So, you're telling me that, in your professional opinion David Stewart was *actually* possessed by a demonic entity?" Wilson said in disbelief. "And subsequent to that, David Stewart and Father Anderson were both somehow... teleported out of the facility to God knows where, and currently, our former psychologist, Dr. Rachel Hoggendorf is possessed by a similar entity. AND... AND... Jesus Christ on the cross, that all of this coincides with the multiple fatalities that we've had happen here and that I'm still actively covering up from the media and the deceased family? Have I got that right?"

"Are we on the record here?" Dravendash asked.

"Does it matter either way?" Wilson replied.

"At this point I guess it doesn't. Yes, that is what I am saying."

"Christ," Carl Bagg said, shaking his head.

"If I may?" Father Gio said from the phone.

"Yes, go ahead," Wilson replied.

"That is but one potential. There are other potentials, but we need to cross them off the list first."

"Such as?" Bagg said.

"Maybe this was an elaborate ruse to break free?"

"Nobody has left the facility. Cameras have confirmed that, as have the secured gate data. Already been triple-checked."

Father Gio held out his hands in a motion that said, *there we go,* as though he'd answered emphatically that they had been transported out of the facility by some unseen force.

"What now?" Darryl asked, letting out a heavy sigh that didn't relieve any of the weight that sat within.

"I think you accept that Father Anderson and David are gone, and you turn your focus to Rachel. If you believe there is any chance of saving her, of getting her back from wherever her mind has gone, you focus on her and you do your damnedest to treat her," Father Gio said. Darryl looked at Carl, both men thinking the same thing – *can she be saved?*

19.

I FEEL LIKE I'M drowning, Darryl. That the real me is being held below the surface and there's no way to fight my way back up for air.

I don't think I can win this battle.

I know you know this is the real me, the Rachel you worked with, and I hope admired.

How did this happen? It feels like I got swept away in a landslide, that a wall of mud came down upon me and I had no time to react, only getting pulled away from where I was a moment ago, and now I'm lost, never to be found.

But I do see an answer, or at least a solution.

A way back to a surface, but it might not be the surface you and I share.

I can taste it.

The bitterness of the ash on my tongue.

Time to answer the call, Darryl.

I wish you well.

*

When Darryl arrived at work the following day, he was unsurprised to find a mass gathering of news vans and reporters. Someone had leaked details, details that should never have been shared with the public.

He suspected it was Father Gio, the man wanting to get out front and discredit all the professionals who worked here. Someone had played a clip of Darryl stating he believed it was a real case of demonic possession and that two people had been transported elsewhere. When he'd first heard the sound bite on his TV, he'd scoffed, wondering what fool had said that. The TV had been on in the background while he made dinner. When the talking head said it was Dr. Darryl Dravendash, he had coughed, choking on the career demolition that had just happened across the airwaves. Bagg had texted him and told him to come to work the next day, to turn off the TV and ignore the onslaught of phone calls he was about to receive. He'd done just that.

The second thing he was unsurprised about was seeing Carl waiting for him just within the doors. He told Darryl that Rachel had disappeared from her cell overnight and was unaccounted for.

"She's gone to wherever David and Anderson went. She told me she would. But I still didn't believe her."

20.

SOMETHING SNORTING NEARBY WOKE Rachel.

She felt the hardness of the ground under her back, which startled her. The last thing she recalled was going to sleep in her cell, the hard floor smooth but uncomfortable.

A snuffling and sniffing came again, the creature grunting in front of her, its snout pushing against her bare arm, tickling across her exposed breast.

Rachel stood, pushing the hair away from her face, wanting to get a clear view of what had touched her.

My hair.

Her hands found her head, fingertips pushing through a full, thick head of hair.

But how?

Looking around, her heart dropped.

As far as she could see in every direction was rolling, forested hills.

She was standing on top of one such hill, taller than most, giving her a view of the darkened land. Looking down at herself, she found she was nude, and not two feet in front of her was an odd creature that grunted and snorted as though it was a mini pig with a shortened elephant's trunk. Her nudity didn't catch her off guard, but it did surprise her to find her nipples were there, despite the vivid memory of the soft buds crunching between her teeth.

"What is going on?" she said. A light snowfall began, which she at first welcomed. As realization hit that it wasn't snowflakes in the air, but ash, a sadness began to devour her heart.

What David had said was true.

She had been chosen and brought over to the world of ash.

The creature, which appeared to lack eyes but did have short, coarse fur all over its round body, rubbed up against her. She knelt, stroking its sides as it pushed against her, and would've continued if not for a sharp pain that suddenly exploded from her lower leg. The creature snorted and scurried away, leaving behind a three-inch long quill sticking out of her skin.

Plucking it out, a tiny stream of blood began to flow. She had no way of stopping it, and as the ash fell faster and thicker, she made her way into the nearby forest, wanting to get out of the stinging downfall.

"Rachel."

She stopped when she heard her name, heard his voice.

David trotted over. His appearance was far different than what he'd allowed her to see in the facility, but it was David, nonetheless. The hoofed feet, hairy, animal legs, and long, curved horns protruding from his forehead made her cringe and look for a way to escape.

"Rachel, my dear, there's nowhere to run. Come, Mother awaits us. We must do as she asks."

He reached out and took her hand, and, to her surprise, she accepted it.

As they started to walk together, she noticed Father Anderson's naked, bloated body at the base of a tree, his head impaled on a branch.

"Oh, don't look at Father Anderson. His kind are not welcome here. A few friends had their way with him, then left him to gaze into the abyss."

She followed David, taking in her surroundings. The ruined buildings, the scorched grass and trees from some previous fire, the bones of the dead spread throughout the undergrowth.

"Look," she heard David say, pointing to the sky.

Tilting her head, Rachel gasped.

A black, cyclical span of stars filled the darkness, churning counterclockwise as though someone was controlling their speed.

"When you look up, this is what you must see, to know that you've been granted access into the black heavens."

A smile came over her face.

After some time, a small fire became visible on the horizon. It grew in size as they approached, and when they were near, Rachel could see the beasts from before standing around it, waiting for her.

She didn't protest or put up a fight when David led her into the middle. She stood, watching as Mother approached, a smile across her haggard face.

"My child..." said Mother.

A tentacled appendage slithered from her body and found its way to Rachel, wrapping around her upper body before finding her mouth and forcing its way in. Rachel's eyes watered as she gagged and choked at the intrusion, which pushed further down her throat. As the tentacle invaded her, David bent her over, entering her from behind. He began to thrust, his claws digging into the tender flesh of her hips. The watching creatures howled and roared, their own engorgement and arousal on full display.

Mother spoke as Rachel felt the knot at the base of David's dick expand and lock into her, his seed pumping in spurts as he came.

"You're one of us, under the blackened sky, as life will grow within, we take this step towards tomorrow together!"

A warmth passed over Rachel, blocking out her brain's struggle for oxygen. She could feel something already taking root inside her womb, already stirring as though it'd been there for months rather than seconds. David remained knotted inside her, stroking her back, his claws opening wounds all along her flesh.

Above them, the stars spun faster, dizzying in their intensity, and deep within the cosmos a single light blinked, letting Rachel know that at last... she had arrived.

END

Afterword

Well.

Here we are.

But how did we get here?

For those who don't know, this novella and my trilogy of novellas that comprise the Father of Lies series, is all based on real events which I was privy too, when I was an observer of a cult I located on the Dark Web. I go into it in more detail in the Father of Lies: The Complete Series release and even more in my memoir The Color of Melancholy, but essentially for four years, I was a non-practicing member of this cult and watched with horror and deranged glee over what occurred there. Horror fiction, at its core, is designed to unsettle the reader in some fashion. This could be through emotional impact, moral greyness, scares, or a growing sense of unease. All of this makes up key components to genre fiction, but often times, the fictional horror we read doesn't hold a candle to the events that happen every day in the real world.

My goal in researching the cult and its members was to bridge that line of fiction and non-fiction, which I hope I've achieved.

Saying that, these works are not for the squeamish and reader mileage may vary.

Which brings me to the writing of this novella.

When I wrote the first draft of this novella, it was solidly epistolary. I had a series of letters back and forth, as well as patient notes and clinical transcripts as well as video transcription to tell the story. But when it was done, I hated what I'd created.

I personally struggle with reading epistolary and that created issues when I went back to work on a second draft. So, I switched it and in some key places you'll still see elements of that mixed media aspect of story design I started with.

As for the narrative 'looseness' in places, specifically who is talking to who etc. etc. Well, now that you've read this, I can discuss it a little because I don't need to worry about spoilers.

The first element here was that I wanted a clinical setting with a strange patient. And I wanted the reader to read it as though it was this patient, David, being assessed and interviewed by our doctor, Rachel.

The second element was that I wanted it to come across that maybe, just maybe, David never truly existed and that this story is all Rachel sharing it, having worked as a doctor who was possessed, first by this 'David' character and secondly by the 'demon' element. Did it work? I think that's for each reader to decide, but when I pitched this one, I pitched it as Come Closer meets A Head Full of Ghosts for a reason.

Because of this approach, I figure results and reviews will greatly vary. Either the reader will get it and love it or not like how I created it and hate it. Either a 5 star or a 1 star. And both are perfectly acceptable responses. As is everything else by the way, including DNF's.

As for the book release itself?

Well, as you might've seen, this one was originally released through DarkLit Press. Then I pulled the rights back and have now re-released it.

Ultimately, things took a turn at DarkLit. Overpromising, underdelivering and contractual failings all led to significant things not being completed or disclosed.

After I announced I was requesting my rights back, I had an outpouring of support which was wonderful.

But what did the future for the book look like once it had been unpublished and was back with me?

I had serious discussions with my wife about what I should do. I had a few small presses reach out (thank you!) and while that was truly kind of them, I focused on two aspects in my decision to re-release this through my own self-publishing imprint, Black Void Publishing.

The first was that there was a lot of momentum from publication day. With that momentum, time was of the essence. Not completely knowing the 'when' of when this one would be able to release again, I wanted to be able to strike at a moments notice. It wouldn't be fair to another press to have to suddenly jump when I said jump so that the book could get back out into the world. But I can do that with Black Void Publishing, so that's what I decided to do.

The second was the strong desire to bring this one back into the fold and work it into the Father of Lies world and mythology I've created. I didn't mind that it was part of the 'DarkLit' series of books with how DarkLit released, but truthfully, I'd prefer this to be within the Father of Lies series of books and let readers experience all of The Black Heavens.

While many still look down upon self publishing, this is where it undoubtedly has its advantages. I control every aspect, from the formatting to the editing, to the cover design, to the release date. Self publishing is akin to the DIY punk movement which I really dig.

Still, I'll thank Andrew, formerly of DarkLit, for believing in this novella and bringing it into the DarkLit family.

Secondly, thank you to David Sodergren for your tireless work behind the scenes for all these years, making me a better writer. I can never thank you enough.

To Andrew Pyper your friendship, support, assistance, and advice have been above and beyond.

A huge shout out of thanks to Kealan Patrick Burke, Duncan Ralston, C.M. Forest, Evan Dickson, and Tim McGregor who gave this an early read and shared some kind words.

Thank you to the cult who allowed me to watch like a fly on the wall. I hope those who truly believed have ascended and can taste the ash.

Thank you to everyone who has read and supported my work.

Greg Chapman – your artwork is phenomenal, and I can't thank you enough for all you've done. You're a great friend, world class author and talented artist. I appreciate you more than you know!

Kristina at Truborn – thank you for working with me through the strange release event!

Linda Jones – thank you for your kindness, compassion and utterly amazing performance with this audiobook. It was a dream to have you come on board and you nailed this one perfectly.

Lastly, Amanda and Auryn. You make everyday that much brighter.

Until we meet again.

ABOUT THE AUTHOR

A MULTIPLE-AWARD NOMINATED AUTHOR, Steve Stred lives in Edmonton, Alberta, Canada, with his wife and son.

Known for his novels, 'Mastodon,' 'Churn the Soil,' and his series 'Father of Lies' where he joined a cult on the dark web for four years, his work has been described as haunting, bleak and is frequently set in the woods near where he grew up. He's been fortunate to appear in numerous anthologies with some truly amazing authors.

His novel 'Mastodon' will be translated into Czech and Italian over the next few years.

He is an Active Member of the HWA.

For TV/Film Rights, please email Alec Frankel at IAG.

LINKS:

Website: stevestredauthor.ca

Twitter: @stevestred

Instagram: @stevestred

Tik Tok: @stevestredauthor

Universal Book Link: author.to/stevestred

ALSO FROM STEVE STRED

Novels

The Stranger

Piece of Me (Sermons of Sorrow Book One)

The Navajo Nightmare (co-authored with David Sodergren)

Incarnate

Mastodon – *nominated for a 2022 Splatterpunk Award for Best Novel*

Churn the Soil

The Color of Melancholy *(non-fiction)*

Novellas

Wagon Buddy (Wagon Buddy Book One)

The Girl Who Hid in the Trees

Ritual (Father of Lies Book One)

Communion (Father of Lies Book Two)

Sacrament (Father of Lies Book Three) – *nominated for a 2021 Splatterpunk Award for Best Novella*

The Window in the Ground

The Stone Door (The Window in the Ground Book Two)

Scott: A Wagon Buddy Tale (Wagon Buddy Book Two)

The Future in the Sky (The Empyrean Saga Book One)

The Bandaged (The Empyrean Saga Book Two)

The Devourers (The Empyrean Saga Book Three)

WE WATCH

Collections

Frostbitten: 12 Hymns of Misery

Left Hand Path: 13 More Tales of Black Magick

Dim the Sun
The Night Crawls In
Of Witches...
Father of Lies: The Complete Series
An Endless Darkness: The Novellas
Into the Darkness: Stories Volume 1
Into the Light: Stories Volume 2

Please enjoy this bonus novelette, 'Claustrum' which also takes place within the world of Father of Lies!

CLAUSTRUM

"Let the blackness take hold and see the stars for what they are."
"And what are they exactly?"
"The cosmic light that guides us to immortality."

*

Moving into a new apartment had always terrified Lacey.

She'd come from an 'unusual' upbringing, and by that, it meant that when she was three, her aunt had taken her without telling her mother and father. The reason she did that was because they wanted to run away to some strange religious commune on the outskirts of the city.

Her aunt had raised her, until an unexpected car accident on the way home from work took her away from Lacey. She was thirteen when that happened, still a child. The authorities had 'looked' for her parents in hopes to reunite them, but Lacey had already known they'd perished at the commune, the stories of the group-suicide plastered all over the news in the days and weeks after it had been discovered.

At thirteen, she was too old to be adopted, too old for a foster family to really consider taking her in, but also too young to live on her own. Magic had struck once, when her aunt had taken her in, and to her surprise, magic struck again.

This time, it was her teacher, Ms. Olson. Ms. Olson – "You can call me Sandy at home, but at school, we should probably keep it formal." – had learned only a week after the accident that Lacey was essentially floating, no home to call her own, no extended family to care for her. And the state was planning on placing her in a facility for those they considered 'left behind.'

Her life with Ms. Olson had been wonderful and together they worked through Lacey's anxiety, trauma, and fears. The most common panic attack inducer for her was the thought of abandonment. She really was without an extended safety net. Lacey had made some friends who she considered close to brothers and sisters, but she kept them at arm's length, not fully letting them into her world. If something were to happen to Sandy, she didn't know what she'd do, and she didn't think she'd make it through another loss.

Then, the inevitable came. She graduated. Got accepted into a college. Moved. At least this move was planned, and it was into the dorms. Sandy made the forty-five-minute drive up every weekend for the entire four years of Lacey's program so the two of them could hang out and stay as close as possible in their relationship. Lacey remained guarded with Sandy being the only person she could just be herself around.

Then, the second inevitable came. She graduated from college. And was offered a position in one of her dream companies. The only issue – it was in the middle of the country and Sandy wouldn't be a short drive away. They discussed Sandy retiring early and moving with her, but both decided that wouldn't do Lacey any good, wouldn't help her to overcome some of her fears.

Sandy explored transferring to teach at a school there and getting her own place, so they could remain close in distance. But once everything was investigated, she found out she'd lose her pension and would most likely have to work for another forty years just to be able to retire. That was out of the question for Lacey. She couldn't let Sandy do that.

So, the only option was for Lacey to move on her own, into a new apartment and start life completely fresh. Which absolutely petrified her.

*

"A blackness has taken hold."
"Drink of it and accept it as your savior."

*

Thanks to the power of the internet, Sandy and Lacey were able to view a few listings virtually, and then a few months before she had to move, they flew out to view those that made the cut in person.

It felt comforting having Sandy there with her, even if it was only a temporary thing and not long from now, she'd be packing her meager belongings and moving out all on her own. Even thinking about that threatened to open the dam and spill the water works of tears that she knew would be coming at some point.

When all was said and done, Lacey decided the second apartment they'd looked at would be perfect for her. A small, two-bedroom unit with a deck that would let her sit on at night after work and enjoy the evening warmth. It only had a shower, no bathtub, but that suited her just fine and the kitchen and living space was an open concept, which gave her plenty of space to put a small table, couch, and wood-block island. She wasn't the best when it came to the kitchen, but she wasn't the worst, and this apartment had the most amount of counter space out of them all. The location was also the best of the three. There was a family-friendly park on the north side of the complex, an outdoor pool within the complex, which was gated and required a card to access and best of all, it was only a five-minute walk from her new job. She had already started to wonder if she might pop home over her lunch break or not.

Before they flew back home, Lacey had paid a damage deposit and the first and last month's rent and a tiny sliver of anxiety faded away. She had a job. Step one. She had a place. Step two of what seemed so impossibly daunting was done. Lastly, step three would be when she *actually* moved, a date that loomed large in the future.

*

"Shall we begin what needs to be done?"

"Not yet. Be patient. The veil will be pulled back and the truth will reveal itself to all."

*

The first week of living on her own proved to be far less frightening than she'd thought it would be.

Lacey had expected an emotional breakdown, either at the airport when she said goodbye to Sandy, or when she was on the plane. Neither had happened. She kept waiting for the other foot to drop once she was in her apartment – *her apartment!* – but it never came. Nor did it come when she finished her first day, purely orientation, which though a bit of a snoozer put her at ease for what the roles of her job were and what her expectations were.

After a hectic week of work, trying to remember what went where and whose name was what, she arrived home at the end of workday Friday, breathed out as though her lungs were bottomless, and a single tear escaped from her left eye and trickled down her cheek.

That was it.

She was out and doing it on her own. All by herself.

Her phone rang, Sandy's face and number popping up on the screen, and she clicked 'ACCEPT,' her adopted mom filling the surface of the smartphone.

"Hey honey! Congrats! The end of week one!"

Sandy's enthusiasm was *exactly* what she needed.

"Thanks, mom."

It had taken a few years of them tentatively building a relationship outside of the school setting before one day, Lacey had blurted out 'mom' when she'd said something to Sandy. They'd both frozen, each contemplating the ramifications of such a word used between them.

"Ok. So, if you feel comfortable enough around me and that is how you consider me, I'd feel very honored if you called me 'mom,' Sandy had said. Her eyes were ringed in tears. This was a moment far more emotional than either of them had expected.

"I would love to call you 'mom,' mom," Lacey had replied, her own tears coming. They'd walked to each other and hugged then, confirming to each other that they both considered each other as mother and daughter.

Thinking about that moment, now, as Lacey walked around her own place in a strange town while talking to Sandy on the phone really confirmed to her just how amazing a mom Sandy was and had always been.

"Do you feel different? More adult?" she asked Lacey, laughing even as the words came out.

"I feel the same, but not like an adult at all," Lacey replied. Movement near the door caught her eye, but she didn't notice anything at first, carrying on with her mom.

They shared a laugh and spent the next hour talking about everything and nothing.

Outside, cars zipped by, and the world continued to turn. Lacey laughed so much her cheeks began to hurt and happy tears streamed down her face.

Once they'd said their goodbyes and Lacey had hit the 'END' button on the call, she went to the kitchen to grab a drink. It was then that she saw something on the floor. A tiny piece of paper, the edges jagged, as though it'd been ripped from a larger piece of paper.

Remembering the movement she'd thought she'd seen, she understood that it was from this piece of paper that had been forced under her door.

Only one word was scrawled on it in pencil.

'*Welcome.*'

*

A week later, Lacey had completely forgotten about the paper she'd discovered. Instead, the week had gone swimmingly, and she'd started two tentative friendships with coworkers, which made her happier than she'd even realized. One of them, Janice, had invited her to come to the dog park nearby, so Lacey could meet her small Frenchie, Pablo. Janice had shown Lacey close to a million photos of her beloved pup starting on Lacey's first day at the job. Janice was in love with the little dog and Lacey was excited to meet him in person.

She'd puttered around the apartment that morning. She caught up on two episodes of a reality show she always watched, sent a few texts to her mom and after procrastinating far longer than she normally would've, she ordered herself a new Bluetooth charging station from Amazon. She'd planned on going to the nearby electronics store to buy one from them, but when she went in, they had nothing compatible with her model of phone. So, Amazon it was.

Packing a few things for the dog park visit, Lacey saw the piece of paper tucked near the knife rack she kept by the door. It was purposefully placed there – at the edge of the kitchen island for use while preparing food, but also near the door so she could grab one for protection if needed. She wasn't totally convinced if a bad guy blasted down her door that she'd be able to grab a knife and stab them, but it gave her peace of mind and that was enough for her.

Finding the note, she went and tossed it in the garbage can, watching as it slowly danced back and forth through the air until it landed on top of the other trash.

Hurrying out, she couldn't wait to meet Pablo and have Janice show her all the tricks the little guy knew.

*

Four hours and a mild sunburn across her shoulders later, Lacey bounded up the steps to her apartment, still in a daze over how wonderful the day had gone. Her and Janice had hit it off even better outside of work, the two chatting and laughing like lifelong friends. And Pablo had been the perfect gentleman, running up to her when she arrived and giving her dozens of Frenchie kisses. She was practically in heaven, watching the beefy little guy sit, roll-over and play dead. He even did a very convincing 'prayer' pose, where, when Janice told him to 'pray for a treat' he rocked back onto his haunches and lifted his two front legs up. Crossing his paws, it looked just like he was sitting to pray, and Lacey loved it so much, she convinced Janice to give Pablo extra treats.

Entering her apartment, she caught a hint of a smell, something mildly rotten. *Gotta take that garbage out*, she reminded herself, setting down her bag and water bottle. She went and tied up the bag, and when she turned to take it down to the dumpster, saw a torn piece of paper near the door. *Odd? I thought I threw that out.* Walking over to retrieve it. Once there, she saw there was writing on it, far more than a single word. Picking it up, she smirked, understanding now that it was most likely from a lonely, desperate neighbor.

'*We should visit.*'

"In your dreams," she said to the paper, slipping it into the trash bag. Heading down to the dumpster, she half expected to discover the writer of the notes leaning at a convenient place to introduce themselves, but, like pretty much every other day she'd lived there, she didn't see anyone else in the hallways.

Returning to her place, she wondered just what the next note would say. *Maybe this is how I meet the man of my dreams,* she said to herself, before retreating to her bathroom to find something to calm the growing annoyance the burns on her shoulders had started to create.

*

"*Fool us once...*"

"*Fool us twice...*"

*

As the next few weeks progressed, Lacey all but forgot about the notes, so focused on work. When a big contract was acquired, her group was brought into the boardroom and the facts were laid out. They'd be working overtime for the next three weeks to get this project wrapped up. In exchange, they'd all receive extra pay as well as a full week off with pay. So, while the thought of how much work was about to be required, Lacey took it in all in stride. She'd get extra cash and an entire week off with pay, which would be a perfect time for her to hop on a plane and surprise her mom with a visit. They'd been talking about when she might get back home, and this would be the perfect opportunity.

The reality of just how much extra work had been thrown at them soon became evident. Lacey arrived two hours early each morning and most days stayed three to four hours longer. After the first week of that chaos, the group collectively decided it made more sense for them to bring what they could with them home at the end of the day.

When she arrived back at the apartment building that night, Lacey wondered if anybody else lived in the apartment complex other than her. *Well, me and the note writer*, she thought, hiking up to her place. She'd still not seen another person. She'd heard someone walking past in the hallways a few times. She'd even heard a door close. And she'd caught a glimpse of somebody leaving through the front door once. But not once had she seen a real *actual* person.

The apartment complex was four levels tall, with six apartments on each level. The main level had a simple entrance, the property management company had a small office where rent could be dropped off, as well as the stairs that led to the upper levels. It seemed like the setup would have had her run into somebody by now.

So, it surprised her when she got to her floor and she saw someone was standing at the far end, looking through the window towards the street.

Going to her apartment, she nervously glanced at the figure, who'd yet to move. She'd expected some sort of acknowledgement that she was there, a subtle look back, or shifting of their body weight, but instead they'd remained transfixed on whatever it was they were looking at outside.

As her key slipped into the slot and she turned the knob, the figure sighed heavily.

"Can I help you?" she asked, wishing she'd not spoken as soon as the words had finished.

"Amongst the black heavens, amongst the cosmic chaos with dust and ruin and flesh."

"I'm sorry, what?"

She tried to unscramble whatever it had been that this person had said, a person who remained facing away from her. She pushed her door open, preparing to step in and leave this crazy person alone, when the door opposite hers opened and she turned.

Standing within the entrance, she quickly averted her eyes when she discovered a naked woman. The woman looked to be close to fifty, with a prominent belly hanging down, almost completely to her knees. Her large, elongated breasts hung on either side of her gut, the nipples turned down, the areolas the size of car headlights. The lady was resting her arms atop her breasts, fingers intertwined as though she was admiring the sunset, not standing naked in the hallway. Her hair had not been cleaned in some time; thick, matted clumps hung around her face. Her eyes were sunken with darkened circle around both. Lacey suspected if the woman spoke, there wouldn't be many teeth within her mouth. A smell had begun to infest Lacey's nose as she tried her best to look at only the woman's eyes or away from her nakedness, but as the smell became a ragged stench, she had to set her bag filled with folders from work down and bring the back of her hand to her nose, stifling a gag.

The woman didn't speak. Lacey thought for a moment she might ask what was wrong with her, especially as she let out a bark of a cough, something phlegmy and approaching puke. Instead, she seemed to be rolling something around within her mouth, her cheeks and lips shifting and undulating.

"From hoof and horn the flock will be summoned, gathered to dance and rejoice!"

The figure shouted the words, spinning around in glee. Lacey saw them spin in her peripheral, but she never turned her head from the woman. That was because, as the figure shouted, the woman began to let something fall from her mouth. At first, Lacey thought it might be chewed up hot dog, but as the chunks fell and a dark red fluid dripped over her chin and mixed with the pink bits, she understood it was the woman's tongue.

"Mam! Mam!" she shouted, wanting to help her but so repulsed she didn't move, the thought of touching any part of the woman revolting.

Pushing her disgust away, Lacey shifted towards the woman when she let out one loud, horrendous noise – 'GAHK!" – and proceeded to lunge towards Lacey. Lacey shouted in surprise and toppled backwards, falling into her apartment. She kicked the door closed, leaping to her feet, and clicking the lock shut and sliding the security chain firmly in place.

As she slumped to the floor, back against the door, she remembered that she'd left her work bag in the hallway.

*

"The property management company insists that nobody has lived across the hall from you for over two years."

Lacey stood, arms crossed, leaning against her kitchen island, trying to process what the police officer was telling her. *It didn't make sense.*

As soon as she'd regained her composure, she pulled her phone from her jacket and called the police. They'd arrived within minutes. Now, twenty minutes since their arrival, Lacey found herself questioning her own sanity.

"I'm sorry to have wasted your time," was all she could fumble out, her eyes unable to rise enough to look at the kind cop.

"Never a waste. You saw something and called it in. Better than not calling it in and something happening that could've been prevented. Do not, and I reiterate that, do not hesitate to call us again if you see anything at all. Understand?"

His tone was soft and gentle and was able to coax her to look at him, her embarrassment still flooding her cheeks with redness. But, when she looked, she saw his face was sincere and that helped to reduce how she felt.

"I will."

"Great. Here is my card. It has my direct number, which if you dial it will call this phone," he held up a cell phone to show her, before clipping it back onto his belt. "I will answer it. 24/7."

"I really do appreciate that."

He nodded, gave her shoulder a firm but comforting squeeze and then as fast as they came, the cop and his partner were gone, and she was alone.

Thankfully, when they'd arrived, they'd brought her work bag in, as she wasn't sure if she'd be able to face the hallway again tonight.

Lifting the bag onto the island, she was thinking she should give her mom a call and the two of them could laugh together over the hilarity of her freakout, when she noticed something sticking out of her bag.

Pulling the jagged piece of paper out, she knew immediately that this was written by the same person who'd slid the previous two under her door. She also knew that person was the figure who'd been standing at the end of the hallway.

'*How divine tongue can taste.*'

*

Lacey became a hermit over the next week, too afraid to leave her apartment. She called into to work, letting them know she was catching something and didn't want to spread it around to the others, so they let her Skype in and virtually participate. She started trembling when one of her colleagues suggested they could bring some soup to help her feel better, with Lacey meeting them downstairs at the main door.

She politely declined, happy when the subject was changed.

At the end of the workday, she stood under the shower for so long, her skin was scorched, redness covering her.

It was when she stood in her bedroom, clad in only a towel, and worked to wrap her hair in a smaller one, when she heard a voice from behind the wall.

"*Accept the chaos.*"

"Hello?"

She should've called that cop right at that moment, she knew better, but she still went to the wall and placed her head against it, turned sideways to push her ear as close as she could.

"*Let the beast suckle at your teat.*"

Lacey jumped away from the wall when a sound like scales across rock came next, coming from within the wall. She tripped over her laundry bin, hair and body towel flying off as she landed on her ass at the entrance to her room. She normally would've laughed at the absurdity of her situation, naked and splayed out from her fall, but the sound of whatever was behind her wall continued. Seemingly growing louder, as though whatever reptilian creature was so big, its body was threatening to burst through at any second.

*

A knock on her door had her scrambling for anything that she could consider to be a weapon. She found a thick hardcover book sitting on her coffee table, a book she'd told herself she'd read but hadn't made any effort to crack open yet. She approached the door, wondering who it was, as she'd not been expecting anyone. She snuck a look through the spyhole and immediately burst into tears, her heart leaping from her chest.

She slid back the chain, unlocked the door, and flung it open, diving into her moms' arms before the woman had been able to even say hello.

"What are you doing here?" she asked once they'd broken the embrace and Lacey had helped her bring in her suitcase.

"Your work was worried about how sick you were, so they called me," she said, eyes darting around the place, looking for discarded tissues and dirty dishes, some of the more common signs of being ill. Finding nothing out of order, she crossed her arms, shifted her weight back on her left leg and eyeballed Lacey up and down.

"Ok, I'm not actually sick."

"Then what's going on? Do you have any idea how worried I was flying out here? And not once did you reply to my texts or answer my calls."

"What? No, I have no calls or texts from you. Nothing. So, I apologize that you were stressed, but anything you sent didn't come through."

Her mom let out a little huff, and pushed past her, going to sit on the couch. Lacey had never heard her mom make that noise before, whether in general or directed at her. She grabbed her phone and flipped through both her missed calls list and her texts. Nothing. She'd been positive her mom hadn't done either, but it calmed her slightly that there wasn't anything there she'd missed.

"See, mom. No missed calls or texts."

She went and sat beside her mom, thrilled that she was here, especially considering how she still couldn't bring herself to leave the apartment. Maybe, just maybe, they'd be able to leave together.

Her mother waved it off, stretching her body as she slouched more on the couch.

"How's work?"

"Don't you want to know why I've been home 'sick,'" she asked, wondering if there was something going on with her mom. She was acting stranger than she'd ever seen her act before.

"Oh, I just figured it had to do with work," her mom said, sitting straighter.

Loud footsteps sounded from the hallway, somebody stomping by before turning and stomping back. Lacey tensed up, sucking in a deep breath. *Was it the note slipper?*

The steps stopped just outside her door.

A soft knocking began, tentative knuckles rapping on the door in a rhythmic pattern.

"Are you expecting someone?" her mom asked. "Or is it for me?"

Lacey's head spun. *Why would it be someone for her mom? Who even knew she was here?*

She sat frozen in place as her mom stood and approached the door. Without looking back, she opened the door and stepped outside, the door closing with a gentle *CLICK.*

"Mom?"

Lacey still couldn't move.

"Mom?"

She couldn't hear any voices from the hallway, which freaked her out. If it *had* been someone for her mom, shouldn't they be speaking? Animatedly excited that she was there?

"Mom –" she paused when her mom's suitcase rocked back and forth. She'd left it near the kitchen island, but it was away from the side. Nothing was around it. Yet, it had shifted. As she watched, the luggage rocked again, and the material at the front bulged and adjusted.

Lacey stepped towards the bag, her internal monologue screaming at her to not go any nearer, to stop there and go check on her mom. But when the luggage rocked again, her hands overrode her mind, and she was unzipping it before she knew what she was doing.

Just hold on a second, she told herself, kneeling and taking a deep breath. *What could be inside this?*

As she started to slowly unzip a rattling sound began, something that sounded familiar, but she couldn't place where she'd heard it before. As her shaking hand undid the zipper and opened the luggage completely, what spilled out was something he'd never expected in a million years, especially from her mom's bag.

Rattlesnakes.

At least a dozen snakes in a ball sprawled out onto the floor of her apartment, their diamond shaped heads and distinct patterned scales writhing and wiggling. The hollowed keratin ends of their tails shook; the symphony of certain death created by the creatures chilling her to her core. Two of the big-headed reptiles darted towards her, eliciting a scream in reply, she stepped back and looked for something, anything to put in between her and the venomous fangs within their heads.

When she didn't find anything within arm reach, she did the next best thing – at least in her mind it was – and rushed to the door, opening it, and quickly going out to the hallway, slamming the door behind her.

To her surprise, there was no sign of her mother anywhere.

Instead, at the far end of the hallway was the odd figure, once again.

"Hello," she said. In response to her voice, the man turned their head towards Lacey without responding.

"Where's my mom?" she asked, voice raising.

"She was never here," the man replied, his voice raspy.

"What? No! She was just here. You knocked, right? She came out to see you for some fucked reason."

The man chuckled, shaking his head. She took it to mean that the man couldn't fathom she thought her mom had been there.

"She was here. Where is she? I won't ask again."

"Or what?" the man asked, turning to face her straight on.

Lacey had to stifle her surprise when she realized she'd seen this guy before. He was always sitting near her workplace, on the street, legs crossed and a small sign asking for change. It'd been a front. He'd been watching her this entire time. But why?

"Who the fuck are you?"

"We've kept tabs on you all these years, Lacey. They wondered what you'd become in this life. What path you'd take and if you'd ever see the truth."

"How do you…"

The dirt that caked his face fell off in little chunks when he smiled at her question, as though she should know the answer and was a fool for being too stupid to know.

"Ahh, little Lacey. How I've missed you. I know you don't remember much from back *then*, when we all lived together and were one big happy family. And then you were gone, and I was left to tend to the sheep and do as Father bid."

"Father? My father?"

The man smiled wider, exposing decayed gums and missing teeth. From the other side of her door the *TTTTTTTTTT* of the rattlesnakes sounded, as though his smile was the switch that triggered them.

"Not your father. *Our* Father. He so blessed he brought the storm and the rain. He led the hoof and the horn and helped us taste the ash."

Before she could reply, the man went to the apartment door nearest. Without putting a key in the lock, he opened the door, pausing before stepping in to look at her once more. Then he disappeared inside, the door slamming shut behind him.

Lacey rushed to the door, grabbing the handle, and turning but finding it now locked. She pounded on the door twice, but stopped, knowing it was fruitless. Turning back to the hallway, she approached her own apartment door, putting her ear against it, listening for the rattle of the snakes.

When nothing came, she slowly opened the door, before she pushed it wide open and jumped back, wanting to be far enough away to avoid a lethal strike from a snake.

Instead, the front entrance was clear. No sign of any snake and to her disbelief, the luggage appeared to have moved.

Against her better judgement, she entered. She knew if a snake bit her, she'd curse herself until the moment she died for being so stupid, but nothing seemed real anymore and after the odd man had seemingly disappeared into a locked apartment, she had a suspicious the snakes may not be what she thought they were. *It's all in your mind. Something is doing this, leading you astray*, she thought as she delicately tip-toed further into her place.

Looking throughout each room, Lacey doesn't find a single snake, nor any sign of the luggage. She steels herself knowing there's just her room left. Entering, her hands fly to her mouth, eyes bulging in terror.

Her bed is covered in the shed skins of the rattlesnakes.

As she watches, each of their rattles rise and begin to rattle.

TTTTTTTTTTTTT.

*

He answers on the second ring.

"Officer DiPietro."

His voice is just as she remembers it, a timber that resonates but a softness that suggests he's there for whomever is on the other end of the line.

"Um... I... uh... look, I don't think you'll remember me, but my names Lacy and—"

He cuts her off before she can continue.

"Lacey, yes of course, what's going on? Do I need to get there ASAP?"

She appreciates that he doesn't question her more or make her feel crazy. Just straight to the point.

"Yes. Yes, please."

"I'll be there in ten."

*

DiPietro was knocking on her door five minutes later.

"Lacey, it's me, Officer DiPietro."

A part of her wondered if it was really him or if this was another *thing* just like with her mom, but she had to trust that it was him, knowing she desperately needed help.

She opened the door a few inches, just enough for one eye to make sure it was just him and that awful hag wasn't hiding behind. Satisfied, she pulled the door all the way open and stepped back, letting the officer enter.

Leading him to her living room, she offered for him to sit on the couch, but he declined.

"What's going on?" DiPietro asked.

"Ok... you're gonna think I'm crazy, but I don't care. I'll tell you what happened and show you what was left behind, and maybe having some real evidence will prevent you from sending me to the psychiatric hospital."

"I promise that won't happen," he said, miming with one hand as he crossed his chest.

At first reluctantly, then with more conviction, Lacey filled in DiPietro about what had taken place. Then, as she neared the ending of her story, she led him towards her bedroom.

"And then, I found these on my bed."

She stepped aside so he could look in without her being in the way.

"Wow," he said. She could see his eyebrows arch, a good sign for that just maybe she wasn't as crazy as she thought she'd been.

"One... two... three..." he counted them off as he approached the bed, right index finger figuratively tapping each one from a distance.

"Six. And no sign of that suitcase anywhere?"

"Nope."

He pulled out his cellphone, taking a bunch of pictures from different angles of the skin. Using a pen from his breast pocket, he lifted a few slightly off the bed, allowing the photos to show that they were truly real snakeskins, not some item photoshopped in or a prop.

"And the rattles, they, what? Just started rattling?"

"Yeah," Lacey said, stepping towards the bed. "They raised up from the bed as those a snake was still within them and made that *TTTTTTTT* sound."

"Wow," he said again.

"Your 'wow' responses are not making me feel any better," she said, trying to chuckle but failing to sound genuine.

"Yeah, you're right. Sorry, not very professional of me. Can I speak frankly? Maybe even slightly off the record?"

"I guess," she replied, a solid pit of anxiety sitting firmly in her stomach. She had absolutely no idea what he was going to say or where he was going with this, but she knew that if he wanted to speak off the record, it wasn't going to be a good thing.

"Ok, so, this apartment building has a significant history of, let's call them 'odd' calls. I didn't know this until I was here last. But when I got back to the station, the boss sat me down and shared that since the day it was built in the late 60's, they've received hundreds of calls. Noise disturbances. Lurking. Trespassing. Attempted break and enter. The usual stuff we get for most apartments. But it's the other cases that he shared with me that made me think you'd be calling sooner than later."

"Such as?"

"You wanna have a seat?"

"No, I'm good. You think I need to take a seat now? Look at my bed?" she said, suppressing a laugh. This wasn't a funny situation and even if she usually used humor to lighten the mood or calm her internal anxiety, this wasn't one of those situations where it seemed appropriate.

"Fair. Over the years there's been reports of devil worship, people disappearing without ever being seen again, and even animal sacrifices."

"That sounds very 'Satanic Panic,'" she said, this time unable to stop a smile from forming.

"Normally, I'd agree. But there's validity in the reports. And from the very beginning, each report noted one thing that across the board that each case had in common."

"What was that?"

"Every single one stated that at some point before the incident that finally forced them to call, they received a note. Either slipped under their door or left in their mailbox."

Lacey felt like the walls were crumbling around her. As though suddenly she found herself submerged under water, the surface too far above her, the air in her lungs slipping out and she was drowning.

"Lacey? Lacey?"

She heard DiPietro's voice, but it was a million miles away. His face came into view, shimmering and fluid in front of hers. It was only when she realized the roof was behind him that she understood she'd fallen to the floor.

"I'm sorry... did I pass out?"

DiPietro hooked an arm under hers and helped her to her feet, the room spinning once she was upright. He steadied her, his body feeling both firm and comforting against her.

"Are you ok?" He asked when her footing was finally found, and she could stand on her own.

"I think so. Everything just kind of hit me when you said about the note."

"I suggested you sit down," he said with a smirk. Neither of them could hold in the laughter after that, which felt good. It felt like a release and as though this was a moment that ended whatever it was that was happening before and from here, she could move on, move towards a solution.

"So, what now?" she asked, after they'd regained their composure.

"I don't think we'll be able to bait whoever is behind this. They might have this place bugged or wired with cameras. I'll stay close by. You keep your phone handy."

"Wait, that reminds me. Before my mother arrived, I heard *something* behind the wall. Something huge. I thought the walls were going to fail. I even thought... it was a giant snake slithering behind the panels."

"Let's take a look," DiPietro said, swiping his cellphone's screen and hitting a saved number.

*

"What do we do now?"
"We watch. We salivate."

*

Thirty minutes later, DiPietro's buddy, who went by the dubious moniker of Sketch, was knocking on her door. Sketch was an ex-con who, once out, had started helping DiPietro. It was a give and take relationship. Sketch told DiPietro about some aspects of what was happening outside of the law and DiPietro looked the other way from time to time when Sketch and a few of his pals were up to no good. Sketch also helped DiPietro when he needed to keep some things off the books. Like removing a wall in an apartment and patching it back up after.

Lacey kept her distance from Sketch, not liking the way the man's eyes roamed over her. She didn't care that he was covered in tattoos or stunk like pot. What she did care about was Sketch waiting for DiPietro to look the other way giving him a potential moment to be inappropriate.

"Bossman," she heard him call out after the noise of removing the wall panel had ceased. DiPietro went to join him in her room, as she waited at her kitchen island.

After only a few seconds, DiPietro popped his head around the corner and told her to come take a look.

She expected that something would be there, but what was behind the drywall still shocked her. The first thing she saw was the grey dirt everywhere.

"I wouldn't touch that," DiPietro said when she made as though she was going to. "Pretty sure it's ash. Could be cremated remains." This caused her to visibly shudder, the thought that people's final remains had been stuffed between the walls physically upsetting. The second thing she saw was the odd assortment of animal appendages. She wasn't overly familiar with all the animals of the world, but it looked like there were goat's hooves, rabbit's paws and a few other dried feet with claws and longer nails.

But the thing that really stood out was the massive snakeskin that Sketch was still pulling from within the wall. It dwarfed the shed rattlesnake skin that remained on her bed. The skin was massive, but while the length of it should've been what scared Lacey more than anything, it was how thick it was. The animal that had shed that skin had been immense and there was no doubt in her mind that she had heard it through the wall just the other day.

"Where did it go?" she asked, relieved when Sketch finally pulled the last bit of length from the wall.

"Not sure," he replied without looking. "There's no where for it to go. Cement on either side here and no openings up or down. Whatever made this should be right here."

DiPietro had a perplexed look on his face. He hovered over Sketch, taking more photos with his phone, the flash lighting up the interior space that Sketch hadn't exposed.

Lacey remained watching. From behind her, an odd sensation began, as though someone had entered the room while the three were focused on the wall.

Turning, she found the suitcase sitting directly in the middle of the living room. She could see a torn piece of paper resting on top.

*

Normally, Lacey would've protested DiPietro's help, but after finding the luggage and the note, she agreed immediately. He was getting her a hotel room for the night, tomorrow they'd return so she could pack all her essentials, and she'd return to the hotel. The victim's assistance fund the police had would help her with the hotel until she could find a new place to rent, but she was leaning more and more towards simply quitting and moving back with her mom. Fuck this shit.

Sketch had patched the wall back together but would still need to return to completely repair it, sanding, painting, and finishing. She didn't care. She wasn't even worried about her damage deposit being returned. When Sketch had left, she'd noticed just how silent he was, which unsettled her. If this place creeped him out that much that was enough for her.

While DiPietro made some calls, she grabbed her suitcase, putting in a few changes of clothes, underwear, a book that she didn't think she'd read, and then went to the bathroom and grabbed her face wash, some makeup, deodorant and her toothbrush and toothpaste. Looking down at her belongings stuffed in the suitcase she felt a tad morose. This was what was important in her life? Just this? A tear fought to escape from the corner of her eye, but she blinked rapidly, returning it to its anatomical prison.

DiPietro cleared his throat, standing at the door of the bathroom. She'd been so focused on her stuff that she'd not even heard him approach.

"I got a swanky place for you for tonight. A treat, from me. Then tomorrow after we grab whatever else from here, you'll move to a mid-level hotel. I wish I was rich enough to keep you at this place longer," he said with a smile.

"You've already done more than enough, and you shouldn't've spent your own money on me," she protested, even as he casually waved it away.

"Ready?" he asked.

She nodded. He reached in and took her suitcase from her, leading the way out of the apartment.

A tenseness rose up but left just as quickly when she stepped into the hallway, expecting to find someone waiting to accost them, but it was empty.

Lacey followed DiPietro down the stairs. He stopped at the lobby, setting her suitcase down.

"I'm at the far end of the parking lot," he said. "Let me go pull the car up. Wait here, I'll be two seconds."

She watched as he pushed through the door and jogged away.

From nearby, a breath was exhaled.

*

"In the land of ash, true believers will not see, nor taste soot, but will experience the light and love of immortality."

"That is why we do what must be done."

"Of hoof and horn."

*

The figure stepped beside her, his stench so foul Lacey gagged and had to spit on the floor. The mix of body odor, dirt and infected rot was so overpowering her eyes watered. As she stumbled, she was able to see that the man had stopped in front of the door, blocking her escape.

"You've seen what needs to be seen, young Lacey," he said. She knew that the figure was the same one she'd seen in the hallway before, but everything about them seemed different, changed. Taller, thinner, dirtier.

He turned, the stunted shift dragging her eyes lower, her gaze falling on the hooves that jutted prominently from below his mud-caked pants.

The lobby spun, the world tilted and when he smiled and his forked tongue darted forth, caressing the plague-crusted teeth, a moan escaped from her mouth, one that to her conveyed fear, but within his eyes she saw he considered it as orgasmic.

"Don't be afraid my dear. Your brother was such a brave and courageous soul. Our flock and Our Father will always praise Brad and what he did for us and what he opened. But we need you to join us again. You were always chosen to taste the ash."

Brother? How was that possible?

"Are you ready to join us? To take my hand, stroke my horns and ascend for all eternity?"

He reached to her, a furry, clawed appendage instead of fingers held out in hope. She looked up, finding his hair had concealed two curved prominences, that looped away from his head before twisting and growing towards the front.

Reality tore in half for her at that moment. She began to scream, clawing at her face, dropping to the floor hard enough to shatter her kneecaps. The man laughed an unhinged laugh as he stepped directly in front of her. As he lowered to pick her up from the floor, a brightness overcame her eyes, forcing her to close them.

*

"We've tried to lower her medication so that she's not so heavily sedated, but I'm afraid with even the slightest change she reverts to this state."

Sandy Olson looked helplessly on through the one-sided glass at her adopted daughter who thrashed violently against her restraints. Dr. Dravendash had been a lifesaver for her daughter, she knew that. She'd heard about him through a mutual friend, after the story about the 'demonic patient' had gone viral. While he waved his hand and scoffed at any of the validity to the story when she'd first asked, seeing the way he navigated Lacey's condition made her believe there was more truth than rumor to what had taken place with the patient the tabloids had named 'David.'

"What would you suggest we do next?" she asked, dabbing at the sides of her eyes with some tissue.

"I think a multi-faceted approach is necessary. If you can manage, a monthly visit would ground her in something familiar. As well, we'll continue to adjust her meds until we find a balance where she's not yelling all the time or a zombie. If we can find the perfect mix where self-harm isn't a worry, I think that's the ultimate goal. And I'll continue with her therapy. Once she understands that she had a hallucinatory breakdown, I think we can contact Officer DiPietro and maybe even have him come for a visit. He's been in contact a few times to ask about her. Those two seemed to connect and he seems genuinely worried for her wellbeing."

Sandy turned away, unable to look at Lacey any longer. With her head shaved and the veins bulging in her forehead, she looked nothing like the girl she'd raised and the woman she'd become.

"I'll contact you in a week or so," the doctor said from behind her. She nodded, not allowing herself to look back. She left the facility, cursing Lacey's mother's name, knowing this was all because of what they'd gotten into all those years ago.

*

"Ascension shall be ours and it'll be more glorious than we can ever imagine."
END

Survived your time in The Black Heavens?

Why not delve deeper into the mythology with this sneak peek of 'Ritual,' Book One of the Father of Lies series!

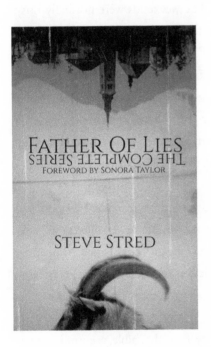

SNEAK PEEK OF RITUAL

1.

MONDAY MORNINGS WERE ALWAYS the hardest for Brad. The sun shone into his room, little particles of dust dancing through the light. He rubbed his eyes and yawned, wishing he was still sleeping. The weekends were normally busy, but with the deadline looming, he'd have to fit in more than normal over those two days. He stood and opened the door of his cheap closet to see what clean clothes he had. He owned three pairs of pants and five work shirts, which let him get through his work week without garnering stares or any snide comments. He grabbed one of the pairs of black slacks and a grey dress shirt and laid them over the back of his plastic outdoor patio chair that sat at the foot of his bed. He went to the washroom and looked into the mirror, thinking back over the weekend.

*

Brad had worked hard to create routine during the weekends. His week was based around routine so he ensured the weekend would be controlled as well. He wasn't a fan of surprises or chaos. He'd pick up the groceries he would need for the week, read his bible, mow the lawn (the blasted grass was growing so fast now, he had to cut it every weekend), and then read more of his bible. That was his normal Saturday.

Sundays brought a whole other mess of busy. Laundry, bible, vacuuming, worship, bible study, soup kitchen, nap, bible, and then America's Funniest Videos. He found while his routine was great, he still needed to relax a bit, wind down some and nothing was better than watching people on tape doing something funny. He'd find himself laughing so hard at his small tube TV that he'd be crying or get the hiccups. He used to enjoy watching stand-up comedy specials but found lately the men were too vulgar and the women spent too much time discussing their feminine problems. He wasn't interested in their sinful ways, so he stopped watching those and focused on wholesome family programming.

Now, with the impending deadline (vigorously circled in red sharpie on his calendar) approaching, Brad was doing double time on the weekend in preparation. This explained why he was moving so slowly this Monday morning.

Last Friday after work, Brad had made the trip to the hardware store and replenished some supplies that were getting low. The group would be happy to see that Brad had completed this task on Friday. It would save them valuable time over the following days. Next Brad went to the art supply store and the candle store. The number of candles they burned never ceased to amaze him. Finally, he went to the dry cleaners and picked up the robes for the flock. He had to make three trips to his car, struggling under the weight of the thick garments.

Normally Brad tried to get to sleep early on Friday nights. His tasks took him until almost nine, so by the time he ate and read some passages, it was pushing midnight. No worries, he thought, all in due time. I'll get the sleep I so deserve. I've done what's been asked of me.

Saturday arrived like a boxer punching him after the bell. It took him a moment to get his bearings, sitting up in bed, sore and swollen. Although he'd never touched a drop of alcohol in his life, he imagined this was what a hangover would feel like. Shouldn't have had all those fast-food burgers so late, he pondered. Too much sodium. Not good, no sir-ee. Feet will be swollen and eyes with be puffy.

The sun had just poked its shiny face into Brad's stark bare bedroom. He did his morning yoga routine, enjoying the feeling of stretching in the nude and felt the tight, scarred skin on his back unknot as he moved. He deserved every lashing he'd ever received, but the skin certainly wasn't too fond of the sensation.

After he had dressed, brushed his teeth, and used the electric shaver to quickly get rid of the short stubble, he made some toast and read through a few verses while drinking some tea. Over the last few weeks, he'd found his taste buds had left him. Now everything filled his mouth with the sensation of eating charcoal, as if each morsel of food had been marinated in a bed of coals. Once he made it through breakfast, it was time to start the day.

This Saturday featured more of the same. Repetition, repetition, repetition. Lawn mown, bible read, groceries obtained and more bible read. He also folded the robes he'd picked up, shined the shoes that matched each robe and sharpened the ends of each pair of antlers attached to the head dress. He marveled at the different thicknesses between the elk antlers and the caribou antlers. The goat's horns weren't as silky smooth as the larger antlers. He found four sets of antlers from animals he couldn't place. He'd make a note to research them later, but the length and curvature had him baffled. Then he went to meet with Father, where he received five lashes. He had indulged in some urges during week, when he'd witnessed a young lady's skirt blow up in the wind. He needed to pay for what he'd done to himself. Father made sure to not strike him hard enough to draw blood, but the welts would sting for some time. More damage to the scars, Brad thought, as he dabbed the area with a hand towel.

"Go my boy and thank you for your honesty. He appreciates your candor."

Brad went home and applied some ointment to his wounds, wincing as they stung. It was only mid-afternoon, so he spent a few hours reading his bible, cringing when a few pages pulled out. He knew he needed a new bible. This one had been read well over 5,000 times, but the sentimental attachment he felt to his current edition made it hard to let go. The leather that wrapped the exterior was so well worn where his fingertips nestled, it was as though the Lord himself had made the copy just for Brad.

Flipping through the pages, he found a few that still had blood splattered on the deckled edges and when he arrived at the Revelation of John, he found entire pages stained a dark red, the words hard to make out. He softly caressed the hardened fluid with his hand, smile on his face, excitement on his breath.

He woke up on Sunday in bed, blood-stained bible still open. He didn't remember falling asleep but as he started his stretching routine, he felt thankful he'd completed all of his Saturday tasks. If not, he would be in for more lashes.

After stretching, teeth brushing, shaving, and his ash flavored breakfast, Brad looked at the calendar with joy. One more week of work before the deadline arrived. Next Sunday was coming fast, the date noted, the preparations in place. Well, almost in place. He just needed to finish up today's tasks. When he was chosen as the anointed one, he was beside himself. First, he was angry and frustrated - WHY ME?! Then he was elated and cried tears of joy - ME? OF COURSE, ME!

He just wished he had some family members left to talk to about this. They'd be proud of me, he thought, tears dribbling slowly down his cheeks.

As the month moved along and the deadline inched closer, Brad knew the flock had made the right choice. He was going to do everything he could to make it perfect. He wouldn't fail them.

So that Sunday, Brad hurried out of the house and began completing his remaining tasks. When he got home, he did his laundry for the week, did the vacuuming, and did some light dusting, before heading to the soup kitchen. At the kitchen, many of the needful who came for lunch daily smiled warmly at him, while some babbled incoherently. A few who were lucid and not drugged or drunk congratulated him on his honor and wished him well. "Thank you," he would reply, while ladling out their portions. He always made sure to stir the soup, not wanting any of the liquid to settle at the bottom. "If you let it settle," his father used to tell him, "They'll taste the difference."

When he was done serving the needy, he helped clean up and then pulled out his trusty book to read for an hour, filling his mind with the Lord's kind words. Then he went and found Father and they spent some time going over the plans. Nothing could be done out of order, and everything had to be just right. Brad knew He would help, but at the end of the day He had no pressure. It was just Brad who'd be put on the spot. Father suggested they meet again each night after work this week, so that Brad would feel comfortable and confident. It would ensure smooth sailing on Sunday. Brad thought that was a fantastic idea, and as Father unzipped Brad's jeans, Brad picked up the swish and lashed himself across the back, only finishing once he was spent.

SNEAK PEEK OF MASTODON

Prologue

JUNE 1ST, 1990

The howling of wind accompanied by the sound of rain brought her back.

She came to in a cave, naked.

Pain rolled across her body as she moved.

This was followed by the throbbing pulse in her head. Reaching to the back of her skull, she felt a goose-egg poking through her matted hair, the area sore to the touch. Her hands shook, her skin wrinkled and cold from exposure. She was shivering, the wind whipping into the dark space where she sat.

She ached all over, unsure what had happened, where she was, or even who she was. Her knees were in rough shape. She wanted to touch the area but was afraid of what she'd find. She was bleeding heavily, and knew she needed medical attention. Her current location suggested that wasn't going to happen.

The pattering of rain hitting rocks grabbed her attention. Looking towards the light source of the cave, she saw the opening of her rocky cage.

She shuffled forward, unable to fully stand. Her bare feet didn't appreciate the bite of the surface, but she ignored it, wanting to see just what type of imprisonment she'd been tossed in.

The entrance to the cave was blocked by thick branches, lashed together by thicker, rough rope. She grasped the bars, pushing and pulling but finding no give. Beyond, the rain continued, accompanied by another gust of wind, the trees that surrounded the cave using their roots to hold firm against Mother Nature's onslaught.

Feeling her eyes well up, she returned to the back wall, shocked by the sudden realization that her breasts were leaking.

Looking at her nipples, she found cream colored fluid dripping out in a steady stream. She cupped the tissue around, applying pressure towards her areola, and watched as more of the fluid trickled out of her nipples.

Why was she lactating?

She tenderly explored her stomach, desperately trying to let her fingertips bring forth some sort of memory, something to tell her what had happened. Her loose skin and belly button told her that something had been in her recently. Her fingers travelled lower, further south, across her dark patch of hair. Once there, she probed softly. Each contact of finger to fold created pain. When she brought her hand up, she saw the tips covered in red.

The child that had been within had been birthed recently.

"Where's my baby?"

She said it aloud, spoke it to the wind and the woods.

Finding no reply, she yelled it, she screamed it, until snot caked her lips and the tears became so cold she couldn't open her eyes.

She pulled herself back against the closest thing to a corner in the cave, wrapping her arms around her legs as she forced them painfully against her engorged chest.

Still, the only noise she heard was the rain hitting rock and the wind whistling through the trees.

As she huddled to generate some warmth, two names whispered over-and-over in her head. Putting one finger to the wall, she began to use her nail to carve them.

LOOKING FOR SOME COLD-WEATHER horror?

How about some with creatures that live in the far north...

Read on to experience the opening chapter of 'Churn the Soil'

SNEAK PEEK OF CHURN THE SOIL

Prologue

UNDER AN ICY SNOWFALL...

Under a clear, blue moon...

The lyrics of the childhood rhyme rang through her head as she trudged through the ankle-deep snow.

Even on frigid days like this, Saska enjoyed being in the mountain air, loved the feeling of the crisp wind as it whipped and pushed against her.

More so, she loved being where she wasn't supposed to be. Beyond the settlement's boundary. She suspected her parents knew, but at thirteen years old there was only so much they could do to control her. Living where they did meant freedom was put above all else, and Saska made sure to remind them of that fact whenever they attempted any sort of punishment. Besides, she thought, it's not like anything actually happened out here.

She stopped a moment, leaning against a barren pine tree to catch her breath and rest her legs. Saska herself was no more than one hundred and ten pounds and she'd guess her snow suit and boots weighed half of that alone. Far off behind her, a large crack sounded, echoing within her head louder than a gunshot. Her head snapped in the direction of the sound as though on a swivel, her heart hammering away inside her chest.

Night was coming.

They'd been told their entire lives that with the darkness came whatever it was that lived on this side of the clearing, that prowled this part of the land. It's not real, she tried to tell herself, even as another branch broke nearby, and the tops of the trees rustled and shook.

The wind bit at her cheeks, the only part of her exposed enough to offer it flesh. She pulled her hood tighter and adjusted her snow goggles to make sure her eyes remained covered. An odd, throaty-barking sound from high above was enough motivation to get her moving.

As the sun dipped behind the high peaks that surrounded the area they called home, the temperature continued to plummet, the air visibly crystallizing in front of her face as she huffed and puffed. She arrived at the edge of the treeline, the hundred-foot gap of open space between her and the village boundary staring back mockingly. A hundred feet from where these trees ended, and their trees began – safety.

She arrived just as the sun disappeared completely and the night's darkness engulfed her world like an eagle spreading its wings to block out the sun.

Behind her something snorted, a sound that resembled a predatory animal laughing. Something shifted through the treetops, moving from branch to branch, leaping towards the girl that had visited the woods and foolishly remained when the daylight left.

Saska looked to her left, up into the trees, and stifled a scream as the shadow shifted and its bulk formed a shape.

She ran.

But that wasn't true.

In her head she was running, sprinting faster than an Olympic sprinter, but the depth of the snow combined with the thickness of her fur pants and the weight of her boots made it agonizingly slower than it should've been.

Behind her, the things emerged from the trees, still shrouded in enough blackness to conceal all but the shape of the limbs.

"Saska, run!"

She could barely make out her parents on the far side of the clearing, her father reaching out to her yet unwilling to take a single step forward, a single step into the space free of trees.

The border.

The space that separated those who lived in the settlement from those that populated the woods at night.

"Saska!"

Her mother, shouting with so much pain and fear that she was shredding her vocal cords. She could barely hear their pleas over her heavy breathing and the crunch of the snow as she struggled to cover the short span of land, only their mouth's moving, and the suggestion of words being formed.

Keep going, she repeated over and over in her head. Keep going, keep going, keep going, keepgoingkeepgoingkeepgoingkeepgoing.

Behind her, something closed the distance between them to within feet, its hideously disfigured limbs covering the space faster than she'd ever be able to, snow or not. A breath that was both hot and cold permeated her thick hood, its face centimeters from the back of her head. It was toying with her, with her parents. She started to cry, knowing she had no chance of making it, no honest hope of surviving. Still, she reached out, stretched her hands towards her father's, even as his eyes and mouth went wide and her parents took a step back.

Pain exploded through her midsection followed by searing sharpness down her lower half.

Even in the darkness she could see the splatter of her blood and organs across the white backdrop of the snow. Her vision blurred and dimmed as she watched her father wrap himself around her mother, shielding her from the carnage. They remained in a ball while the creature took its time with the body. The second thing from the woods had stood back, stopping halfway across the opening. It watched its kin begin to root around in the trespasser's body cavity before it turned and fled.

Saska's parents remained. They didn't attempt to be quiet, knowing nobody from the settlement would come to see what was going on. Not until morning, at least. And if they didn't cross that unseen line, the creatures wouldn't even look their way.